ROAD TRIP WITH THE ENEMY

THE SWEET WATER HIGH SERIES

KELSIE STELTING

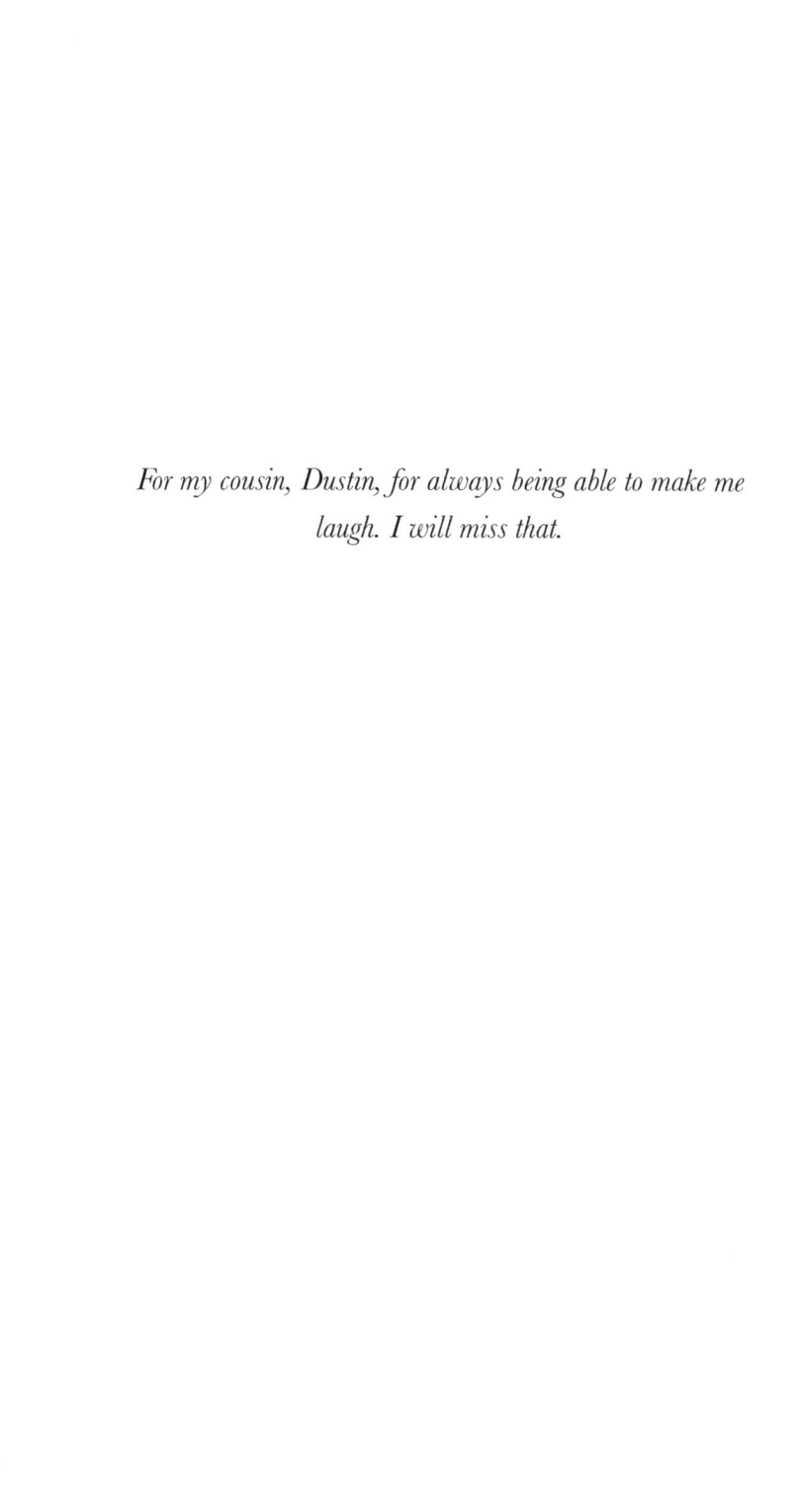

For my cousin, Dustin, for always being able to make me laugh. I will miss that.

Copyright © 2019 by Kelsie Stelting

All rights reserved.

This is a work of fiction. Names, characters, businesses, places, events, locales, and incidents are either the products of the author's imagination or used in a fictitious manner. Any resemblance to actual persons, living or dead, or actual events is purely coincidental.

No part of this book may be reproduced in any form or by any electronic or mechanical means, including information storage and retrieval systems, without written permission from the author, except for the use of brief quotations in a book review.

Cover design by Victorine Leiske.

Editing Sally Henson and Tricia Harden.

For questions, address kelsie@kelsiestelting.com

 Created with Vellum

INTRODUCTION

Welcome to the town of Sweet Water, NC.

1 town. 1 school. 12 sweet romances.

CHAPTER ONE

There was one date I'd never break. Every Saturday morning, I went to the comic book store, bought something from the indie corner, and drove across town to the saddest yet happiest place on earth. I'd been doing it for the last four months, now that my brother couldn't.

Every morning, including Saturday, Liam sat at the dining room table to watch the sun rise over the Cape Fear River. He said he wanted to count how many colors of orange there were in existence.

The hospice house looked like any of the other buildings lining the river, but this one had a keypad for entry and smelled like cleaning supplies. Inside, it could have been a home, if not for the hospital equipment in each room, the widened doorway to allow wheelchairs through.

I went inside, washed my hands at the sink by the door, and greeted his nurse in the kitchen. "How's he doing?"

From here, his shoulders looked a little smaller. Like he was a ten-year-old for once.

"He's having a hard day," Ms. Louisa whispered.

I turned to her, to the plate of chocolate chip pancakes topped with strawberries and whipped cream that he would only eat a few bites of. Our eyes passed a message we couldn't say out loud.

My own shoulders sagged, but I tried a smile bright enough to match the sky, colored with every shade from indigo to pastel pink.

"Hey there," I said, stepping closer to the dining room.

Liam turned in his wheelchair and smiled back, the pale light reflecting off his skin. "Three hundred and twenty-four."

I rolled my eyes because if I showed him how much I wanted to cry, my visit would be doing more harm than good. "You sure? This one looks a lot like one-twenty-seven."

"No, this one's special." He said it with such certainty, I'd be crazy to doubt him. His eyes flicked to the comic in my hand. "What did you bring me?"

I held it up. "Only the most obscure and ridiculous running comic you've ever seen."

His tired smile got wider, and he reached for the book. "*The Running Runner*? Who comes up with this?"

I shrugged and dropped into my chair at the table, inhaling deep to smell all the delicious food. "Ms. Louisa fixed us up good today."

As if on cue, she came in, all bright and cheery. "I sho did. Your favorite, boo."

His eyes glanced over the food and went back to the window. "I'm not hungry."

"You sure you don' want none?" Ms. Louisa asked.

He shook his head again. "But you know Syd's going to eat all of them anyway."

We laughed, and I started dishing myself some food. But truthfully, eating was the last thing I felt like doing.

My brother, Greg, had been a stronger person than me, visiting Liam almost every other day and always coming back home in a better mood.

Maybe because he didn't think of how little time we had with him. These precious few minutes we got to be alive in the grand scheme of the universe.

For a while, Liam and I sat in silence, watching the sun slowly wake up the city. Even though people sped through their day, the river and the sun were always the same, in on some secret joke while the rest of us rushed around.

Once all the orange was gone from the sky, Liam turned his wheelchair to face me, his pointed face all business. "How are you feeling?"

"Fine." And yes, it struck me as odd that he was asking me that question. "Nervous, I guess. Twenty-six miles is a long way to run."

He folded the comic book to his chest and leaned in. "Did you know it takes about a thousand-ish steps to run a mile?"

I tapped the step counter on my wrist. "One thousand, seven hundred and four."

"Which means it will be about..." his lips tightened as he thought.

"Forty-four thousand steps," I finished. I'd already done the math.

He nodded. "And the fastest someone has ever run a marathon is like—two hours. That's shorter than a Harry Potter movie." He shrugged, like it was no big deal.

Of course he and Greg got along so well. Greg with his unshakable, cavalier confidence. Liam with his straightforward view of the world. Spending time with him was almost like having my brother back.

Almost.

I chewed at my lip.

"You don't have to do it, Syd," Liam said. "I know the marathon was Greg's thing."

I shook my head and put my hands on Liam's knees. He told me once that Greg was the only person who ever touched him there aside from the aides and doctors. The amputations made everyone else uncomfortable. Even his parents.

"I am running this marathon," I said. "For Greg." And then I put my thumb under his chin and looked in his tired eyes. "And for you."

If Liam could fight osteosarcoma, I could run a race. I would do it if it killed me.

Footsteps sounded behind us. Liam's mom smiled at us. "What's the count?"

Liam told her.

"And the new comic book?"

He held it up.

She came closer, dropped a kiss on his forehead. "When's Jere coming?"

That name dug its claws into my heart and squeezed, but I evened my expression. It could be someone different. "Who's Jere?"

Liam turned his eyes away, refused to make eye contact.

I looked to his mom for answers, but her eyes were on the doorway. On Jeremiah Dermot.

And the river was inside my ears, rushing water over my brain, making it impossible to think, to hear, to understand.

Liam looked up at me, all wide-eyed and innocent. "He said you haven't talked to him since January."

My head darted from Jeremiah to Liam to Liam's mom. "I..." My mouth was dry. Too dry. I swallowed. "I've got to go. I'll see you next Saturday," I said to Liam. "With pictures."

And then I left, because Jeremiah wasn't just the last person I wanted to see. He was my enemy. For as long as I lived, I would never forgive him for all he'd taken away from me.

CHAPTER TWO

My house was supposed to be a safe haven, but nowhere was safe when the memories lived inside my mind. Half of me had been erased here.

As I walked down the halls of our house toward the front door, changed for my last training run in Sweet Water, I saw the photos missing from the walls—the blank spaces where frames used to be. There was a photo of me when I was a baby. One from my parents' twentieth wedding anniversary. A few of grandparents and aunts and uncles. But none of my twin brother. They were all gone. Like him.

The day after his funeral, my mom put it all

away. Dad was too busy at work to even notice the changes.

So here I was in this house that made his absence so pronounced I felt it with every single step I took.

I missed his photo on the mantle most—our senior pictures used to sit side by side. Now it was just me, smiling like I wasn't months from the worst news I'd hear in my life.

I reached for the door, but instead of being able to slip outside unnoticed, my mom called to me from the kitchen.

"Sydney, come in here."

I closed my eyes for a second and left my hand on the door handle. Maybe I could pretend I didn't hear her.

"Sydney," she yelled, louder.

I let go of the handle and walked through the living room, past her and Dad's packed bags. Past the proof that their marriage was crumbling and they saw an intensive marital counseling retreat as the last chance to fix something we all knew would never work.

No amount of money they threw at their marriage would be enough. Because when you have an almost-done puzzle, you don't see the

CHAPTER 2

whole thing. Your eye goes straight to the piece you lost.

I stopped in the dining room, where my parents sat at opposite ends of the eight-person table. Dad had a stack of envelopes in front of him—paperwork, bills, the usual. Mom had a single cup of coffee and her laptop opened to her version of the news—Facebook.

"Hey," I said.

The blue light reflected in her eyes as she took in a photo of the neighbor's new golden retriever. Finally, she closed the window and looked at me. "Are you sure you don't want us to drop you off at the bus? There's still time for us to drive you there."

Dad flipped from one piece of mail to another. "Only because your mother insists on getting to the airport two and a half hours early."

Her lips tightened. "Sydney?"

"I'm fine," I said. "I need time to get some last-minute packing done anyway."

What they didn't know was that I was not fine. That I was not going on my senior trip with the rest of my class. That I had an entirely different plan altogether. And if they knew any of those things, they would not be leaving for the airport in half an hour. They would not be leaving me.

Mom nodded. "Right."

The screen changed back to the dog, and Mom began typing in a comment.

Papers crackled as Dad set down yet another letter and moved to the next.

I rubbed my arm, waiting.

My parents and I existed in awkward silences.

Eventually, I broke it. "I'm going to head out for a run before the spring break crowd gets going," I said, jabbing my thumb toward the door.

Dad nodded and glanced up at me without really seeing anything. "See you next Sunday."

Mom pulled her gaze away from the screen to stand up, and now her eyes were drowning me. I knew what she saw. My brother's dark brown eyes. His bright red hair, just a shade lighter than hers. His light skin smattered with freckles. His lips that were just a little too thin. She wasn't seeing me at all.

But then she pulled me into a hug, and she felt frail against me, her weight loss the most apparent it had been in months. We'd all lost something. She lost a little more.

CHAPTER 2

"Goodbye," she whispered, her voice cracking.

And even though I knew she wasn't talking to me, I said it back. And then I managed those three words that seemed to be harder to say than ever before. "I love you."

She ran her hands over my hair, down my ponytail. "Call if you need anything."

"I will," I lied. And then I turned and walked past the bags, past the missing photos, and out of the house.

At first, I walked. We lived half a mile from the beach. Jeremiah's family lived right on the water. I had to get going so I could finish early without the risk of running into him. But when I reached the sand, the last thing I wanted to do was start on one of my last training runs.

Instead, I sat, a little too close to the shore. I dared the ocean to come closer, to swallow me whole and lap away my pain.

Instead, it ignored me.

I laid back on the sand, shifting so it would become the perfect shape for my body. For a while, clouds passed, and seagulls crowed, but the pieces still didn't click into place.

Jeremiah had been at the hospice house,

visiting Liam. Liam knew who he was. And they had talked about me. It didn't make sense. Why had he been there?

But I knew why. Because Greg wasn't here, and someone had to visit Liam.

And then I got out my phone.

I read the same text I read every day. Not from my brother, but from Jeremiah.

Jeremiah: I couldn't stop him. I'm sorry.

Today, I deleted the message.

CHAPTER THREE

There was a place in our house where my brother still existed.

My room.

I kept photos of him on the walls. On the mirror. And in a chest at the foot of my bed.

Today, after my run, I opened the chest. When Mom was cleaning out his room, I saved what I could. Some clothes. Some photos. And everything from his backpack.

I lifted out the wrinkled paper, a flyer about the marathon in New York City, raising money for osteosarcoma research, and looked at it the way Greg must have. His dark brown eyes would have lit up—not the transparent way blue eyes did, but in a deep, glittering kind of way that made you wonder what was beneath the surface. I wondered how often Liam came to mind as Greg ran. As he planned the trip.

Volunteering for children's hospice had changed Greg. He felt things more deeply than most people. Cared more than most people.

He'd registered for the race last year. But now I was going to run it for him. No matter how long it took me to reach the finish line.

I put the paper in the bottom of my suitcase, covered it with clothes. I reached into the chest one more time and got my favorite picture of Greg—one of him crossing the finish line during a cross-country meet, the tape breaking across his chest.

He'd looked so alive, the wind he'd created flowing through his hair, his mouth open in a wide smile searching for air, every muscle in his legs tensed for that final push.

I rubbed my thumb over his face. Life could change in a second. In the time it took to make a decision. Every decision counted.

I put the photo in my bag, and as I zipped it closed, I promised, "I'm running this for you."

I carried the suitcase to my car, along with a sleeping bag, some pillows, and a cooler full of food. Not being eighteen yet would make this trip a lot harder, but not impossible.

Finally, my car was loaded. Music drifted all the way from the beach—the spring breakers were in full force, and it was my turn to go on a trip of my own.

I stared up at our house, at Greg's window he used to sneak out. For the last four months, that window had been a gaping hole, but it didn't feel like something was missing now. Just foreign, like a house I used to live in when I was a little kid. Familiar, but changed.

Maybe it was just me.

I turned away and got into my car. Everything had fallen into place. My parents were gone. The weather was clear along the entire east coast. Everyone would think I was on my senior trip. It was like the universe had planned this trip for me. Like my brother was laying out the steps so I could finish his.

I looked at the pages of maps I'd printed out, of the beautiful places along the way where I'd take photos for Liam. I wanted to make the most of this trip for him.

Maybe a piece of me needed this too.

I steered my car down the black asphalt away

from the coast. Each line that passed under my car left me feeling lighter, freer. Every place in Sweet Water had a memory, but I could already feel them drifting away, being replaced with a purpose.

I was doing something. Going somewhere. And soon I'd get to drive away and never come back if I wanted to.

The levity that spread throughout my chest—I'd live for that.

As I pulled onto the highway, I turned up the radio, rolled down the window, and let the wind chase the stale air from my car. All of it had to go.

If this feeling kept coming, I'd be floating the marathon, dancing across the finish line.

But my car had another idea.

Metal screeched in the engine, jerking the vehicle to the right. The heat dial on the dash went to red, and smoke rolled from under the hood. I slammed on my brakes and pulled to the side of the Interstate, horns blaring at me as I went. This couldn't be happening. My car had to work. I didn't care if it didn't get me back. It just had to get me *there*.

I hopped out of the car and went to the hood, desperate to make this work. To pull some mechanical knowledge from my brain, though I had none. Smoke poured from every crack, and I stepped away, biting my lip.

My eyes burned, and I swiped at them with my forearm. This wasn't the time to panic.

I had to come up with a plan.

I couldn't call AAA. They'd report it to my parents.

I couldn't book a last-minute flight. I didn't have the money to do that. If I used my emergency credit card, my parents would get a notification and be in New York before I even landed.

Going to a mechanic would cost money. Plus, I'd actually have to get my car to one, first.

I got my phone out, scrolling through the contacts. There had to be someone. Some fairy godmother who could get me on my way. There had to be.

But every name I passed just reminded me of how much I'd lost when my brother died.

Friends I didn't talk to anymore. Boys who wouldn't come close to dating me. Family it was too hard to see. Family who wouldn't understand or lived too far away.

I passed Greg's name. The one I hadn't been able to delete, even four months later.

He would have been my call. He would have been here, no questions asked. My lips trembled, and I covered my mouth with my hand, willing them to be still. But they ignored me. I slid down against my car on the side facing away from the road and put my head in my hands.

Greg deserved for me to cross the finish line. Liam deserved this.

It couldn't be over. Not this soon. Not before I even had a chance to leave Sweet Water.

"Sydney?"

I shook my head. I knew that voice, and it was the last one I wanted to hear, it's owner the last person I wanted to see me break down.

But I looked up, right into the most expressive brown eyes I'd ever seen. "Go away, Jeremiah."

His brows furrowed, bringing a line to his perfectly smooth face. "Are you okay?"

"Yes," I lied.

"Do you need a ride?"

"No."

He stared at me.

"Someone's coming to get me."

"That's dumb," he said. "We're both going to the same place."

Something in me snapped back to reality.

Maybe the part that couldn't stand to be this close to Jeremiah.

I glared at him. We were going very different places.

My car made a knocking sound.

Jeremiah's eyes widened, and he ran to the car, getting into the driver's side.

I ran behind him. "What are you doing?"

The engine died as he turned the car off and looked back at me. "You want your engine to seize up?"

I folded my arms across my chest and stared at all the cars driving by, oblivious to us. Of all the people to stop, it had to be Jeremiah.

"How far away are you parents?" he asked.

"Just a few minutes."

He stared at me. "You're lying."

I jerked my head back, feigning disdain. "What are you talking about?"

Those brown eyes swept a pattern toward the sky and back to me. "You do the same thing as Greg when you're lying. Your nose crinkles, and your eyes flit to the ground."

I flinched at hearing his name out loud. And at the memory of his expression. I'd seen it a million times growing up. Just never knew I was mirroring it.

He closed my car door and leaned back against the vehicle. "Spill."

I glared at him, then spun on my heel and started walking. Where, I didn't know. Maybe to the bus stop. Or a place where I could get an Uber to the bus station. Maybe I could get lucky and there would be a bus leaving in time. Maybe they would let me buy a ticket without ID.

But Jeremiah caught up to me, keeping pace with his legs that were even longer than my lanky ones. "You're not going on the senior trip, are you?"

I refused to make eye contact.

"Woah, little Miss Perfect, ditching the senior trip?" He chuckled. "You're getting it wrong though. You're supposed to skip the boring stuff. Not a trip to Nashville!"

"Yeah," I said. "Riding on a bus with a bunch of people who either feel sorry for me or pretend I don't exist sounds like a ton of fun."

"She speaks!" he said, and I made a mental note not to do that again.

"Sydney," he said. "Syd."

But I wasn't talking anymore, definitely not to him.

"Sydney!" He jogged in front of me, catching my arms in his grip. "What is going on?"

I looked down at his hands, wanting him to let go.

He held on just as tightly. "Is this about Greg?" he pressed.

And hearing that name spoken out loud again, by Jeremiah, undid me. Something inside I'd been holding on to so tightly broke, right along with the floodgates behind my eyes. I sagged, and now, his hands were the only thing keeping me up.

"Syd," he said, alarmed, and pulled me to his chest. His hand found my hair, stroking down the back of my neck. "I miss him too."

But Jeremiah couldn't miss him. Not like I did.

I pulled back, trying to catch my breath and wipe at my eyes. Trying to be oblivious to what the people on the road were thinking as they drove by. What did they make of the handsome guy with the gangly, crying girl just a few feet from a smoking car?

Jeremiah looked away from the road, toward a strip mall across from us, but I could tell he wasn't really seeing it. "He was going to run a marathon over spring break, in—"

"—New York," I finished. "I know."

Jeremiah eyed me, then my car, like he was seeing the situation for the first time. "You're not..."

I twisted my lips to the side and gestured at my mess of a situation. "Not now. Unless I can find a bus ticket to get me there in time."

He folded his arms over his chest. "That won't be necessary."

"Yeah?" I asked. "And why's that?"

Jeremiah grabbed my hand and started walking back toward our cars. "Because, you're riding with me."

CHAPTER FOUR

I stared at that white monstrosity he called a vehicle—the latest Jeep with all the add-ons money could buy. But all I could see was Greg sitting in the passenger seat, his arms straight in the air with the wind separating his fingers and me in the back seat with them, soaking in the heat of summer.

The idea of sitting where he used to sit felt wrong, on so many levels.

But having Jeremiah's hand holding mine was even more erroneous.

I pulled my arm away. "What are you talking about?"

He stared at me. "I'm driving you to New York."

"Are you kidding me?" Of all the cruel jokes to play, this had to be the worst.

Jeremiah's eyes were all business, though. "Senior trip never would've felt right without Greg. Now I can... I dunno"—he scratched his neck and stared at the cars driving by—"do something that actually matters."

"Stop it," I said, anger flaring my nostrils and making my hands fly through the air. "Even if you wanted to—which I don't believe for a second you do—even if you wanted to, we'd have to sit next to each other, in a car, and spend the week together, and we both know we can't do that."

"Why not?" he asked. "You can't set your feelings aside long enough to get a free ride to New York? You know how much this marathon means to Liam. How much it meant to your brother."

My mouth hung open. He was using Liam and my brother to goad me into getting his way? "How dare you," I managed. "You have no idea—"

"What? I have no idea how much you hate me?" He hit his chest. "You think I don't see it every time you look at me? Or better yet, every time you don't? We used to—"

"It doesn't matter what we used to be," I said.

"You're right," he said, taking me by surprise. "It matters what I am to you now. I'm someone willing to give you a ride. Are you going to take it?"

I chewed on my cheek.

He turned those eyes on me, and they caught me, made everything around us freeze. "Please, Syd? Let me do this."

A low humming sounded in my ears, clouding out everything around me. Was I really saying yes to a road trip with my enemy? With someone whose bad decision cost me the only person I had in this world who would always be there for me?

But when I looked in his eyes, I knew my answer.

I had to go to New York.

I had to run that race.

For my brother.

For Liam.

For me.

I cringed and started toward his car. "Let's go."

We stopped at my trunk, and he eyed the sleeping bag. "What's that for?"

I picked it up. "I can't exactly rent a hotel room."

He grabbed it from me and put it back in the trunk of my failure of a car. "I can."

His eyes told me he wasn't in the mood to argue, and I wasn't up for the fight. If he wanted to use Daddy's credit card to give me a good bed to sleep in before I attempted 26.2 miles, that was fine by me.

So instead, I picked up my backpack, he grabbed my suitcase, and we got into his Jeep. But now that I was sitting so close to him, his arm leaning on the console, I wondered if this had been a horrible mistake.

One that was too late to take back.

CHAPTER FIVE

*H*e sped onto the highway, past my car, and as we topped the overpass, I stared down at the expanse of blue, at the blurred line where it met the sky. Greg. I was doing this for Greg. And Liam. And a road trip—even with Jeremiah—would be worth it every single time.

Wind blew in through the open top, whipping my ponytail back, cooling me from the warm spring sun and humid North Carolina air. Greg would have loved this.

A pang hit my chest as I realized Liam would miss out on experiences like this, with the open road and no parents, no rules. I got out my phone and took a picture for him. I wanted Liam to feel like he was here, even though he couldn't be.

My heart clenched. Even right next to Jeremiah, I felt so alone. My parents had no idea where I was—where I was going, but it had been like that ever since the funeral. We were three separate ships, floating on the ocean until the waves ripped us apart or wrecked us together.

Their therapist thought their marriage had a chance.

I had my doubts. And hopes.

They had a plan already for if the retreat failed. I would start at Duke in the summer program right after graduation. Mom and Dad would pack up the house, divide their things, and then go their separate ways. Mom wanted to get away from her pain. Dad wanted to be away from Mom.

I opened my backpack and got out the scrapbook I was working on for Liam. And ultimately his parents. They'd loved Greg just as much as Liam did.

When I flipped to the page with Greg's senior photo, Jeremiah glanced over, but he had the sense not to say anything. His lips just quirked, bittersweet, and behind his sunglasses, I could see his eyes crease at the corners.

For a second, I wondered what he was thinking, if he was in as much pain as me, but I stopped that right away. I barely carried the weight of my own grief. My own guilt. Carrying his would surely crush me.

Instead, I stared at the picture of Greg. Of his soft eyes and the smattering of freckles and his smile that was always higher on one side. And I poured the story of our senior photos onto the page.

You might not see it, but there's a mud puddle a few feet back. Greg's grinning like that because he just threatened to make me eat a mud pie. And you know he meant it. When we were your age, we'd make mud pies in the backyard where our dog dug holes. We used to add "ingredients." Grass and stuff like that. He always knew how to have fun. He loved having fun with you.

I closed my eyes against the page, against the memory, and leaned my head back, hoping the wind could carry my thoughts away.

Of course it didn't, and I realized I didn't want it to. My memories of Greg were the best things I had left of him.

I turned to the next page, ignoring Jeremiah turning his head toward me so slightly he thought I couldn't see him.

This was a photo of both of Liam and Greg,

splashing in the ocean together. I wrote carefully on the paper, blinking quickly so my tears wouldn't join the saltwater in the photo.

I'm so happy your doctor let you and Greg go to the beach that day. I'm sorry Greg told you that sharks eat shorts. That was a dumb joke. And I'm sorry the seagulls took our sandwiches when we weren't looking. But you got the full beach experience. Greg told me that was one of his favorite memories.

That had been one of mine, too, seagulls and all. It brought a smile to my face now.

I used that momentum to turn to the next page, but I wished I hadn't.

It was a photo from the homecoming dance of Greg, Jeremiah, and me. Greg was in the middle, as usual. It always seemed like we were three points of a triangle, linking back to Greg. He felt even more absent now that Jeremiah and I were together.

Jeremiah didn't pretend not to look this time. "That was an awesome night."

I scoffed. "For you maybe."

"What, not a fan of harmless pranks?" He laughed.

"I wouldn't exactly call putting a worm in my purse a 'harmless' prank," I said.

"You know it was all—"

"I know," I said. "His idea."

His smile fell, almost imperceptibly. "Yeah."

He turned the music up louder, and between that and the wind, conversation was impossible. I welcomed the silence.

That was, until my phone started ringing.

CHAPTER SIX

"My mom's calling!" I yelled.

"What?" Jeremiah shouted.

"Pull over," I said. Ever since the accident, she panicked if I didn't answer my phone right away.

The car jerked, and he crossed a lane of traffic to take us to the exit. I let it ring, but I knew if I didn't pick up soon, Jeramiah and I would both be in trouble.

"Hurry!" I yelled.

"I'm going twenty over. Calm down."

I shot him a glare. My skin crawled with every vibration of the phone, every second that passed without being able to hit answer.

The second we hit a gravel parking lot by a restaurant, I hopped out of the Jeep and answered the phone. "Hey, Mom?" I tried to make my voice seem casual. Not breathless and terrified like I felt. "I thought you'd be on the plane by now?"

"Are you okay?" Worry that was only one step away from hysteria colored her voice. "Your class sponsor called and said you missed the bus."

I squeezed my eyes shut. Seriously? What was the point of that whole speech about being on time and not holding up the class if they were just going to call my parents right away?

"I...don't feel good," I said. "I just threw up."

"Oh no, honey. I'm coming home right now."

"Don't!" I said, way too fast. "Don't," I repeated, more calmly this time. "Look, I'll be fine. Just a stomach bug. Your...thing with Dad is more important."

The airport loudspeaker echoed on her side of the phone. Final boarding call for Nassau.

"Go, Mom," I said. "I'll be fine."

"Fine, but I'm calling Aunt Karen to come stay with you."

My stomach plummeted somewhere beneath my feet. "She lives three hours away, Mom. I'll be fine on my own."

"You might be fine, but I'll feel better if she's with you," she said. "I love you."

"You too," I managed.

Jeremiah sauntered around the car and squinted at me. His sunglasses were gone, tucked in the visor. "Everything good?"

I shook my head, using all of my strength not to fall onto the ground. "She's calling Aunt Karen. What am I going to do?"

"Krazy Karen?" he asked.

"That's not a nice nickname," I said.

He shrugged. "That's just what—"

"—he called her," I finished. I nodded. "What do I do?"

"I mean, can't you just tell her you have a friend coming to look after you?"

"I could." I sighed. "If I had any."

His brows came together. "What do you mean? You can't ask Fiona or Jamie to cover for you?"

I shook my head. "They're both seniors. And Mom would just find out anyway. You know she doesn't trust teenagers anymore."

He frowned. "Why don't you just—"

My ringtone sounded, and we both stared at the screen. Aunt Karen.

"Any bright ideas?"

He stared at the pavement, his jaw working, and shook his head.

I closed my eyes, gathered myself, swiped my thumb across the screen. "Hello?"

My eyes met Jeremiah's, and I hated how much hope I saw there. He needed this trip too; I could feel it.

"Your mama called me in a panic," Karen rasped, probably between cigarettes she chain-smoked. "What's goin' on, darlin'?"

"I'm not feeling well," I said, using my best sick, sad voice. "I think I caught a stomach bug."

"Mhmm," she said. "Now tell me the real truth."

My eyes widened, and I stared at Jeremiah.

"What?" he mouthed.

"She knows," I mouthed back.

The color drained from his sun-kissed face.

"I'm waiting," Karen said.

"I—" I sifted through my thoughts. I had to find a way to make her understand. She loved Greg just as much as the rest of us. "My brother signed up for a marathon before he died. My parents said no, but I need to run it for him."

The line was silent for a long while except for

the clicking of her lighter, the drag she took on a cigarette. "Oh honey, bless your heart."

I cringed, waiting.

"You want me to lie to your mama," she said.

"No," I said. "I want you to help me live out my brother's last wish."

"I can do that." She paused. "But only if you let me come along so I can cheer you on."

CHAPTER SEVEN

I hung up the phone, and Jeremiah stared at me. "What did she say?"

"She said she'll keep our secret." I leaned against the car.

He grinned, his eyes showing even more joy than his mouth. "You're amazing!" He picked me up and spun me in a circle, and for a second, it was like old times—laughing, joking, celebrating together, but then I remembered it was not old times.

We were on our way to New York so I could run a marathon Greg was supposed to for a little boy who didn't have near enough life left in him. And now Karen was going to ride along with us.

He set me down, and I stepped back, straightening out my shirt.

"Don't get too excited," I said. "She said she's coming with us."

"No way." He crossed his arms. "No. Doesn't she have a job?"

"She probably called in."

"Well, she can't come."

"What's our other option? She calls my mom and tells on me?" Desperation colored my voice. Jeremiah had to know how much this mattered. "I have to run this race."

He turned away from me, running his hands through his hair. "Fine." He turned back. "Fine. But she's not smoking in my car."

"Fine!"

Without another word, he started walking toward the building.

"Where are you going?" I asked.

"I'm starving."

I stared up at a rusted sign. Green Corner Café. "You want to eat here?"

He was already halfway to the door. "I'm going in."

My eyes darted between him and the Jeep. I had two choices: sit outside on black leather in ninety-degree weather or wait in a place that made me question whether my tetanus shot was up to date. But at least it had air conditioning.

Inside it was.

I grabbed my bag from the Jeep and went inside. Jeremiah was already sitting down on a green pleather booth, happily chatting with an older waitress. How did he do that so easily? It seemed like everyone was his best friend from the get-go. Maybe that was part of the problem.

They caught sight of me, and Jeremiah waved me over.

The waitress grinned between the two of us, wide and toothy. "You got yourself a looker."

I couldn't tell if she was talking to him or me, but I needed to nip this in the bud. "Actually, we're not—"

"—not in any rush," Jeremiah said. "You can come back in a little while."

I gave him a look and sat down. My legs rubbed over the cracked pleather that had been duct-taped together long ago. "What was that all about?"

He lifted the menu and shook his head. "No need to bore her with backstory."

I raised an eyebrow.

"Look." He met my eyes. "That woman thinks we're two people going out to eat. On a date. Happy." He shrugged. "I don't mind living in a world where that's a possibility. Even if it's just pretend."

No matter how much I wanted to, I couldn't argue. I wanted to live in a world where my life wasn't forever changed by loss, colored by grief. Where my brother was still my best friend and Jeremiah was a cute guy we hung out with. But that wasn't reality. Wishing for something that didn't exist made real life that much more painful.

My mouth formed around the word "what," but I couldn't get it out. The idea of us together was what led to Greg's death.

Now, it was cruel to even imagine.

"Stop," I finally said and picked up a menu, even though my stomach was churning.

"Syd, I—"

"I said stop," I repeated, blinking back tears.

"Ready?" the waitress asked, all business now. Her hair had somehow become more frazzled in the last five minutes. Granted, there were only a few people here, but I didn't even see a cook behind the kitchen window.

After we ordered, she walked away, and now

we had no menus, no drinks, no rolled silverware to distract ourselves with. My hand twitched to my pocket, thinking my phone would be a good place to stare. Better than the thinning table laminate.

Jeremiah rested his elbows on the table, and his shirt pulled against his shoulders. "I—"

The door burst open, and a man I could only describe as scraggly walked in. His wrinkled mouth moved, mumbling incoherent words over and over again. He looked like some of the guys that sometimes dug through trashcans at the beach.

Jeremiah's eyes softened as he watched the man cross the worn carpet and drop into a booth across the room. The kids at the table next to him shot a straw wrapper at the guy's head.

My stomach sank.

Jeremiah turned to me and shook his head. "You good here?"

I nodded. "Why?"

His lips quirked to one side. Then he stood up and walked to the booth where the man was and sat across from him, started talking.

The man's entire stature transformed, like Jeremiah had brought him back to life.

Too afraid to confront Jeremiah, the kids ignored him, on to staring at their phone screens and devouring baskets of food.

When the waitress went to Jeremiah's new table, the man smiled even wider, a toothless smile full of joy. Jeremiah was getting him food.

For a second, I felt Jeremiah's eyes on me, but I trained mine on the table.

Soon, my food arrived, and I tried to get lost in eating the fuel I'd need for the challenge ahead. Even though I'd been training, I didn't know what it would feel like to be running the steps my brother was supposed to. How would the first mile feel? The last?

It wouldn't be easy, but I knew it would be worth it. Running was straight forward. This trip with Jeremiah? Not so much.

What did it mean that I couldn't stop thinking of Jeremiah sitting with the man? Of the fact that he'd been visiting Liam this entire time?

CHAPTER EIGHT

One thing I'd learned was that thinking could drown you, bury you under thoughts so dark there wasn't a light bright enough to shine your way out. That's what kept me going since Greg died, putting one foot in front of the other, keeping my mind busy so I didn't have time to think.

But as Jere and I drove down the road, the thoughts wouldn't stop. And they weren't like the devastating ones about my brother. They were about us.

Feelings I'd quashed so long ago were back, stronger than ever, and all I could hear was Jeremiah saying he wanted to pretend we were together.

The whole thing seemed so trivial.

So why couldn't I stop thinking about it?

A new song played on the radio, and it shot straight to my heart.

Greg's favorite song. "I Lived" by One Republic. He listened to it before every big moment—on the way to cross-country meets, before the ACT, getting ready for dates.

I closed my eyes and pretended he was here with me, on the open road with the wind washing over our faces, baptizing us with freedom and possibility.

At the chorus, I turned to Jeremiah and saw him smile.

He glanced at me. "He loved this song."

A smile found my own lips, the kind of smile that's happy and sad and confused, all at the same time. "He did."

"He loved you, you know."

I looked down at my hands, picked at my fitness tracker. "I know."

The car shifted to the right, and I looked up to see Jeremiah taking us off another exit.

"Where are you going?" I asked, reaching into my backpack for my map. This wasn't the right exit for Norfolk where Aunt Karen lived.

"Somewhere special."

I looked around. This highway didn't seem different from the one we were on before, really. But the farther we got away from the last road, the sparser our surroundings became. We were enclosed now by lush fields interrupted by the occasional stand of trees.

"You're *not* going to get us lost, right?"

"Sydney Thane, is that a threat I hear?"

I shook my head. "I don't hear you denying it."

He laughed, the first real one I'd heard from him in a while. Not the one he made during the school day for everyone else, the one that tried to convince them he was okay. This new sound made me feel lighter.

"I'm not going to get us lost," he said. "I wanted to show you something."

I sighed. He wasn't going to tell me where we were going. And I wasn't going to waste my breath arguing with him. Instead, I watched our surroundings change and took a few pictures for Liam's scrapbook. The trees thinned out to patchy grass, and then to that big blue expanse I couldn't get enough of, no matter how much time I spent in the sand.

Jeremiah pulled over to an empty parking lot and stopped the car. "Come on," he said.

I reached over to unplug my phone, and he put his hand on me so softly, I couldn't help but look in his eyes to see if they held the same regard as his touch.

They did.

"Leave it," he breathed. "This is a no-phone beach."

Why did I feel so lightheaded? I took a breath. "What if I want to take a picture?"

He shook his head, one side of his mouth quirked. "Didn't you know? The best memories are kept right here." He tapped my temple.

Even after his fingers moved away, I could still feel his touch, scrambling each of my thoughts.

"Okay," I said, only because this wasn't one of Liam's designated stops. I peeled myself from the leather seat and got out. Even though I'd been breathing fresh air all day, I sucked in a deep breath. Nothing smelled as good as saltwater.

Jeremiah started down a dirt trail toward the beach.

This beach wasn't as nice as the one in Sweet Water, behind Jeremiah's house. Here, the sand was coarse, dotted with scraggly grass and rock.

But it was empty. I couldn't see anyone, no matter how much I strained my eyes.

Except Jeremiah. From here, I could watch the languid way his runner's body moved, sure of each step. He seemed to fit into these surroundings. Peaceful, beautiful, and relaxed.

"My parents used to take my sisters and me camping here," he said.

"You went camping?" I didn't even try to hide my disbelief.

He smirked. "I've been a time or two." Rocks crackled under his feet as he stepped closer to the water. "Before Dad got transferred and stopped taking time off." An edge colored his voice that hadn't been there before, but he was in the water now, searching the ground.

I slipped out of my tennis shoes and stepped on the rough beach, careful not to tread on anything that could hurt my feet. Twenty-six miles with a sliced-up foot? No fun.

The water lapped up to my ankles, slightly colder than it was at home, but just as refreshing.

Jeremiah picked up a smooth rock and skipped it over the waves. "You still going to Duke?"

I shrugged and started looking for a rock

myself. "That's the plan." Honestly, I hadn't been able to think about it since January. When you lose someone, you stop making plans. You can barely see through your pain long enough to make it to the next day. "You?" I asked.

"Yeah." He dumped a round rock into the water, sending a splash nearly to the rolled hem of his pants. "What're your parents going to do without you?"

"I could ask you the same thing." We were both the last children at home now.

He barely masked the sadness that hit his visage, trying to seem cavalier. "Probably just work more."

I nodded, stalled. Talking to Jeremiah used to seem so easy. Now, I found myself grasping at straws, trying harder than ever to find something to say. This ocean might as well have been between us for how far apart we felt.

"What did you used to do on camping trips?" I finally managed.

He smiled, just a little bit, and pointed to a spot where the sand met scraggly grass. "We used to set up two tents over there. One for Mom and Dad and one for us kids—or sometimes we did girls and boys. And then we'd build a fire out of driftwood. I thought it was the coolest."

I imagined Jeremiah as a little kid, the blue and lavender flames reflected in his eyes. It sent my thoughts in directions I didn't understand.

"We'd bring the jet skis and play on the water or build sandcastles or see who could find the best seashells."

"That sounds nice," I said and skipped another rock. This one barely skimmed the water before going under.

"It was the only time we ever got our parents to ourselves, you know? Every other time they were distracted by things more important than us." He toed the sand. "I was going to take Greg here sometime this summer."

I started walking down the beach, gazing at the sand and shells in front of me. "He would have loved it."

Jeremiah's hand grabbed my own, and I turned to face him.

"I hope you love it." He looked at me, not faking a smile, not putting on the show he did for everyone else, and it undid me.

Suddenly, I was pre-January me, looking at Jeremiah and hoping for once he would see me back. That I would be more than his best friend's sister, someone he could see as more.

The butterflies in my stomach told me maybe he did.

The pain in my chest told me it was too late.

CHAPTER NINE

The night of that party, Jeremiah begged me to come out with him and my brother.

He said that since I was a senior I shouldn't spend my last New Year's Eve in high school watching '80s rom coms. He said I needed to live a little and quit dreaming of becoming the next Molly Ringwald.

I didn't know whether it was the fact that he knew who Molly Ringwald was or that I just wanted to go wherever he was, but I said yes. Of course, I said yes.

And that decision cost my brother his life.

The first thing we did at the party was take shots. They said I had to. That it was a rite of passage. Mostly it just burned. And tasted bad. But I tried it.

And then my brother started making the rounds, hanging out with his friends, saying hi to people, making the girls feel special. I still remembered the way Jeremiah's eyes looked when he took my hand and asked me to step outside with him. They looked like melted chocolate, and I wanted as much as I could get.

Stupid.

I followed him out the back door, down the porch steps and around the side of the house where we were hidden by a row of bushes. He sat down against the stucco siding and pulled me down with him. It didn't feel like he was treating me like his friend's sister. He was *seeing* me. And not looking away.

Those melting-chocolate eyes turned to my lips, then met my gaze again. It was cold outside, but I couldn't tell with his legs next to mine and our fingers still laced together.

Then his head was tilting, leaning closer, and I wasn't smelling saltwater, but his breath, sweet and minty—more intoxicating than anything else that night.

When our lips met, it wasn't fireworks. It was

explosions, bombs, flooding, a full-on hurricane crowding out every thought I had in my mind. I ran my fingers through his hair, gripped his shoulders, let his hands curl around my waist and pull me closer. I had to get closer. I had to get more.

I didn't know why we broke apart, but we did, and we stared at each other, shocked—not only at the fact that we kissed, but that it felt like *that*.

Did regular kisses feel this way? I didn't know.

I just knew that it was him and me, and I never wanted us to leave this spot covered in magic.

His eyes were wide as he looked at me, but all I could see were those lips. The ones that made my body think it was a massive nerve ending, just waiting for his touch.

"Happy New Year," he whispered.

"Happy New Year," I whispered.

And then he stood up and brought me back inside.

We'd already counted down the seconds to the new year by the time a cop walked into the party with my dad and told us Greg was gone.

Before we realized the cost of a kiss.

Now, right in the middle of nowhere, Jeremiah was looking in my eyes like he was searching for something—an answer maybe, but I didn't have one for him. I didn't have any for myself. What did you say to someone like Jeremiah? What words could do justice in a moment like this?

"Syd?" He didn't say it like we were at the beach. He said it like we were at Greg's funeral. Sad and scared and hurting.

I looked away from the pain, turned my gaze to the only steady thing around us. The ground. "What?" I asked.

He sighed, took a step closer, and his sandy feet came into view. Then his hand reached out and fell at his side. "I owe you an apology."

My heart wrenched, and suddenly I felt naked, vulnerable, like a lightning rod in the middle of a thunderstorm. I met his eyes, only for a second. "Don't, it's—"

"No," he said. "I need to say this." He tipped my chin up so I had to look into his eyes, see the torture waiting there. "I've been wanting to say it since—it happened." His head tilted away, and his Adam's apple bobbed with the force of his swallow. "Greg never should have wondered where we were. He wanted me to wait and ask you to prom, but I couldn't. And it cost us too much."

Jeremiah's eyes blazed, broken, and he curled

in on himself, smaller and weaker than I'd ever seen him before. We were like two pillars, destined to stand apart but bearing the same weight.

Part of me wanted to go to him, but I couldn't, rooted by my own grief. My voice cracked. "I wanted to go with you." I fluttered my eyes toward the sky. "And I've regretted it every day since." My grief outweighed the embarrassment. "It's my fault."

He shook his head. "Greg knew better. He knew not to drive."

My eyelids fluttered. "He wasn't thinking clearly. We should have been there—"

"We should have. But we can't go back in time. We only have now. And I think we're messing it up." He gestured between us. "Do you think he would want us to be like this? We're worse than strangers, Syd. We're..."

"Enemies." I finished.

"I want not to be." His lips trembled.

My heart jerked toward him, and the words were falling out of my mouth. "Me neither."

Before the words had completely left my lips, Jeremiah had closed the distance, covered me in his arms.

"Will you forgive me?" Jeremiah breathed into my hair.

"I want to."

We stood like that until all our tears had left our eyes and joined the salty ocean air.

We were alone.

But not as alone as before.

CHAPTER TEN

We sat down together in the aftermath of his apology and my almost forgiveness. This new, strange feeling washed over me. Like if I wasn't holding on to anger, who would I be?

I worked my fingers through the rough sand, tried to focus on that feeling instead. I liked the ocean best from the shore, with the ground firm underneath me when my future felt anything but solid.

Jeremiah sighed and lay all the way back beside me, his fingers laced behind his head. Close enough for me to feel his energy. Far enough that we couldn't touch. Without my anger, the space between us was like a vacuum, just waiting to be filled with something. I just didn't know what.

"Lie down," he said. "The clouds look amazing. There must be a front coming in."

Slowly, I sat back and tried to see what he saw. "The weather's supposed to be good this week." The clouds overhead were long and puffy, like they were barely hanging on to each other in the beachy breeze. If I kept my eyes on them, I could watch their trajectory across the sky. No matter how much they wanted to stay by the water, they'd get sucked away, just like the rest.

"Are you nervous for the race?" he asked.

Thankful for a new, lighter topic, I shook my head. "I've been training for months now."

"I know."

I twisted toward him and raised an eyebrow.

He shrugged as best he could with his hands behind his head. "You run right in front of my house. At six in the morning. Every day."

My lips twitched. "You've been watching me."

"Maybe a little." He smirked, then his expression sobered. "You run like him, you know. Heavy footed. And you swing your arms too much. You might have a promising career standing in front of a car lot."

I dislodged my hand so I could hit his shoulder, and he laughed.

"You're just jealous you couldn't catch him," I said.

"Hey, I beat him a few times."

I raised an eyebrow.

"Okay, once."

Both of my brows went up this time.

"I still think that timekeeper was off."

"Sure he was." I smiled and looked back toward the sky. It was getting paler by the minute. Soon we'd hit sunset. We needed to find something to eat. Somewhere to sleep.

"Twenty-six miles is a long way, though," Jere commented.

"I've been through worse."

He knew what I meant.

A wave crashed toward the shore, coming just close enough to tickle our toes.

"Tide's coming in," Jere said.

I nodded.

He nodded.

And we lay there a while longer, lost in our own thoughts. Together, but alone, not knowing what this meant.

Eventually, the sun tipped the water's edge, and I shivered.

Jeremiah stood, helped me up, and we walked toward the car. I got in the passenger side, but Jeremiah went back to the trunk and brought me a heavy blanket.

"It's colder at night here," he said and spread the quilt over me. His eyes smiled at me as his hands smoothed the fabric over my knees. Even with layers of the patchwork around me, I couldn't ignore the heat sparking from him.

I turned my eyes down. "Thank you."

"Of course." He lifted his hand, and suddenly, I was cold, even covered up. I tried not to think about what that meant. Because if it meant anything, I was in trouble.

This was Jeremiah. My brother's best friend. The guy who had broken my heart before we even dated. Who'd cost me my other half. I'd never be able to see him without seeing that too.

CHAPTER ELEVEN

Before we left, I called Mom to tell her goodnight. She sounded sad underneath the cheery act she put on for me. Something in my gut told me their trip wasn't going as well as she'd hoped. As I'd hoped.

When we said goodbye, Jeremiah started driving back down the road, toward the Interstate. I didn't even bother with the GPS, now that I knew he was familiar with the area. It was so dark outside compared to Sweet Water, though. At night, I could always count on streetlights and headlights. Out here, my vision quickly gave way to black. I couldn't even see the moon, only a small ring of light hidden behind rows of thick gray clouds.

We were still on a country highway when his Jeep started slowing down and the engine faded to silence.

I turned my head to him. "Why are you stopping?"

As he slowed down, he twisted the key a few times, trying to get the engine to turn over. "No, no, no, come on," he pleaded.

My back stiffened as I took in our surroundings. Pitch-black nothingness. "What?"

He pressed the heels of his hands over his eyes and spoke into his forearms. "We ran out of gas."

My eyes widened. "You're kidding," I said, even though I knew he wasn't.

He might have used a few choice words.

I might have too.

"Why didn't you get gas at that last town?" I asked.

"Maybe I got distracted." He jumped out of the Jeep and paced beside it, his phone flashing in the darkness.

I stayed quiet while he made the call. Told AAA we were out of gas. "You can't come sooner?" He sighed. "Fine. We'll be here."

He hung up and leaned against the car,

looking at me with a pained expression. "They're coming."

"When?" I asked.

He cringed. "In three hours."

"You're kidding," I said again.

He wasn't.

I got my phone out of my pocket, dialed a number. "Karen?"

"Don't tell me you're backing out," she said, trouble in her voice.

"We're out of gas," I deadpanned and shot Jeremiah a look. "God knows where we are."

"How far are you from me?"

"Maybe an hour?"

"Send me a map pin. I'll be there as soon as I can."

"Thanks." I hung up. "Aunt Karen's coming." Lightning flashed through the sky, followed by a crack of thunder loud enough to stand my hairs on end. "We should put the top up," I said.

Jeremiah cringed even worse than before.

"You don't have the top."

He shook his head.

"You're—"

"I'm not kidding." He shook his head. "We can deal with a little rain."

A panicked flutter started in my chest. "But Liam's scrapbook...our phones."

He stuck his hand out. "Here. I'll put it in the trunk."

I shoved off the blanket and handed him the scrapbook, along with my phone. I wished I had brought something—a waterproof jacket, an umbrella, anything. But all I had was this stupid quilt.

Sprinkles started from overhead, bringing out the curls in my hair. In Sweet Water, this rain would have been warm, not refreshing at all. But here, it was verging on cold.

"Come on," Jeremiah said, "I have an idea." He walked to my side of the Jeep and opened the door.

"You want me to get out and stand in mud?"

He shook his head. "Nope. Give me the blanket."

"How chivalrous of you."

He rolled his eyes but took it and squatted to the ground. Before I knew what was happening, he had disappeared under the Jeep with the blanket and was yelling up at me. "Come down here."

I gazed toward the sky, searching for who

knows what. It didn't last long before a big, fat droplet landed in my eye and I had to blink it away.

"Fine," I muttered and began my descent, finding myself face-to-face with those beautiful brown eyes and Jeremiah's warm body.

CHAPTER TWELVE

This was the problem with Jeremiah. He was too *likeable*. Being his friend was just easy. Greg had been the same way. Maybe that was why they found each other. They never bought into all the high school drama that seemed to eat up everyone else's time.

One time, this kid literally threw up on me during cross-country practice. We were four miles from the school, on one of our running loops around town. There was nowhere to go, and I wasn't about to run around shirtless.

Without even thinking, Jeremiah had taken off his shirt and handed it to me.

I stared at him, my stomach turning.

"Put it on," he'd said. "Or I'm gonna barf." Then he spun his finger around.

So I did. I turned around, in the middle of the city, and put on his shirt. It was damp. And it smelled like him. I still had that shirt at home somewhere. Did it mean something that he hadn't asked for it back?

He probably didn't mind shedding his shirt in the hot North Carolina fall and running around with girls gawking at him. But he didn't have to, and that was the point.

Just like he didn't have to drive me all the way to New York.

And now, we were stuck under a car, in the pouring rain, in the middle of the night, letting his Jeep's interior get soaked and waiting for my aunt to come save us.

I blinked at him. "I'm sorry," I said over the sound of rain pounding on the pavement.

He shook his head. "Don't be."

"Seriously, you wouldn't be here if it weren't for me."

His hand reached out and touched my cheek, only for a second, but the feeling lingered long after he pulled back. "I've been wanting to spend time with you. I just didn't think I'd have to trap you under a car to do it."

A corner of my mouth lifted. "That sounds a little murdery, Jere."

He laughed. "I gotcha where I wantcha."

I rolled my eyes. "Now I'm gonna eatcha."

He laughed again, and the sound hit my ears, softer than the time before. I realized how much I had missed his laugh.

He shifted and rested his head on his arm. "Would you rather smell like a skunk for the rest of your life or have everyone you meet smell like a skunk for the rest of your life?"

I let out a surprised laugh. "What kind of question is that?"

"A good one."

I shook my head, then rested on my own arm. "Everyone else, that way I wouldn't be the odd one out. They'd be too busy smelling each other to ever notice me."

"Hmm." He nodded. "Good choice. Your turn."

I looked anywhere but at him. At those eyes that were dark but somehow shining. "Would you rather...drive for a day or fly for a day?"

His eyebrows came together. "Fly. What kind of question is that?"

I shrugged.

"You can do better. Go again."

"Seriously?"

He went cross-eyed and stuck out his tongue. "Does this look like a serious face to you?"

I couldn't help it. I laughed out loud. "You're ridiculous."

"You're stalling."

I smiled. "So what if I am?"

"Go."

Finally, an idea came to me. "Would you rather drive an awesome car or have one with a roof?"

"Touché." He laughed. "If it gets me time alone and an actual conversation with Sydney Thane, I'd pick a car without a roof every single day of the week."

My heart swelled within my chest, pressed against my ribcage until it hurt to breathe. Why did being with him feel like this? Why couldn't we just go back?

I shivered, the chill hitting my bones.

"Are you cold?" Jere said.

I nodded, even though the shiver hadn't been entirely due to the weather.

He opened his arms and lay on his back. I scooted over, careful not to hit my head on the Jeep's undercarriage. Eventually, I found myself lying on his chest, warmth radiating through me.

And I let myself pretend that this could work. That my heart hadn't been torn into a million pieces, that my parents weren't on the verge of divorce, and that this entire trip didn't hinge on Krazy Karen coming clean.

It could have been minutes or hours, but eventually, I lifted my head and looked at him—at the way his lashes came together in a dark fringe, at the curve of his nose and the slope of his cheekbones.

His lips spread into a smile. "Are you staring at me?"

My cheeks heated, and I couldn't believe steam wasn't pouring off of them. "Maybe."

His eyes fluttered open, and he looked at me through his lashes. "I don't mind."

I felt that pull again, the same one from New Year's Eve that made it seem like Jeremiah and I were two poles of a magnet, destined to come together. Incapable of staying apart.

My eyes drifted closed, and I leaned closer. Close enough to feel his breath ghost across my face. Closer.

Lights flooded us, and I jerked back, bumping my head on the car's undercarriage.

A car door shut. "Hand check!" Karen called.

Jeremiah let out a sigh, so quiet I almost missed it.

"We're here," he said and started scooting out.

Whatever moment we had, it was gone. A heavy feeling fell somewhere between my heart and my stomach. How had I let myself get that close to Jere? How could I stay away?

CHAPTER THIRTEEN

Karen had a lit cigarette hanging out of one corner of her mouth and a full gas can in her right hand. I turned my eyes toward the dark, misting sky. *Beggars can't be choosers. Beggars can't be choosers.*

She filled Jere's gas tank and patted the side of his Jeep with her bony hand. "Not too shabby, huh, kid?"

Jere put on his most flattering smile. "Thanks Kra—Karen."

I barely stifled a laugh and gave her a hug. "Thanks for getting us."

"Anything for my favorite niece."

"I'm your only niece."

She laughed. "Spunky as usual."

I shook my head. "So...to your house?"

She nodded. "You riding with me or him?"

My eyes darted between the two of them, the rock and the hard place.

"I'll ride with you," I said. Hello rock.

Jeremiah's eyes were unreadable. "I'll follow you."

The second I sat in Karen's car, I was enveloped by the smells of cigarette smoke, cats, and some kind of flowery air freshener. My stomach curled. Suddenly, getting wind whipped and sitting a couple of feet from Jeremiah didn't seem so bad.

Karen craned her neck and looked in the rearview mirror. "Man, that boy is a looker."

My cheeks heated. "Karen! He's my age."

"And?" She winked at me. "It's like bein' on a diet. Look, don't touch."

"Gross."

She cackled. "How's the drive been?"

I shrugged. "You mean, other than getting stranded and having to take shelter under a Jeep?"

"Those're the parts of life worth livin' for, sweetie," she said. "Be spontaneous sometimes."

"Pass." I stared out the window and bit my knuckle.

"How's your mama doin'?"

I shook my head. "The truth?"

"That bad?"

"Yep."

"And this 'retreat'?" she said. "You think it'll fix anythin'?"

"I don't know." Moisture built in my eyes as I told her my naked truth. "I hope so."

She reached out and patted my knee, then gracefully changed the subject. "So, a marathon, huh?"

"Yeah."

"Not bad, girl." She smiled.

"How's your job?" I asked to get us as far away from the topic of my life as I could. Karen loved her job as a motorcycle saleswoman and could go on about it for hours.

"Fine," she said.

"That's it?"

She shrugged. "Mind if I smoke?"

Yes. "No."

She rolled down the window, letting fresh, damp air wash over us. It was marvelous. Until she started smoking.

Which reminded me.

"Oh," I said. "Jeremiah said no smoking in his car."

She cursed. "I knew there had to be somethin' wrong with him."

∼

Karen's apartment smelled exactly like her car.

Jeremiah wasn't good at hiding his reaction to it.

Karen was good at ignoring him.

"That's the cat's room." She pointed at one beat-up wooden door. "That's my room." She pointed at another. "I can set up an air mattress in the cat's room, or you can sleep on the sectional?"

Jeremiah and I glanced at each other and said at the same time, "Sectional."

Either way, we had a problem. We'd be sleeping on the same couch, in the same room. At least this way we wouldn't have to lie side by side. I could even have my feet pointed toward him.

"No hanky-panky," Karen said with a wink. "At least none that I can hear."

I pointed my finger at my mouth. "Gross."

She laughed. "G'night, kiddos."

"'Night," Jeremiah said, still recovering from her comment. After the bedroom door shut behind her, he muttered, "You're telling me Krazy Karen isn't a fair nickname?"

I shoved his shoulder.

He laughed.

Then we both looked at the stained tan couch with two ends that weren't really long enough for either of our tall frames.

"Are you sure we can't sleep in your car?" I asked.

"It's still pretty wet," he said. "We can get a hotel room?"

I shook my head. "We can't make her mad."

His chest lifted and fell. "I call the left side." He kicked off his shoes and flopped onto the cushions. With his knees bent, there was just enough room for me to lie on the other end without touching him.

I sighed and lay down.

A loud meow sounded from the other room, and Jeremiah jerked.

The absurdity of it all hit me, and I laughed. Then Jere laughed. And we were laughing together.

CHAPTER 13

And then Karen was laughing, and it was a little less funny. Or maybe more.

"Goodnight, Syd," Jere eventually said.

"Goodnight."

And even though there were plenty of things around to keep me awake, the one thing that was running through my mind was Jeremiah and me under his Jeep and wondering what would have happened if Karen's headlights hadn't split us apart.

CHAPTER FOURTEEN

"Wakey wakey, eggs and bakey," Karen called.

I blinked my eyes open to see her in a visor, matching track suit, fanny pack, and rolling suitcase. On the opposite end of the couch, Jeremiah was slowly stirring to life.

"What time is it?" he asked, rubbing his eyes.

"Oh-five-hundred," Karen said with a salute.

I flopped back down. "Why are you waking us up?"

She grabbed my hand and pulled me back up. "Everyone knows road trips go better when you leave early. Now get ready to go. We can stop and get a biscuit on our way outta town." She clapped her hands together.

CHAPTER 14

Jere and I gave each other a look.

"I'm gonna pretend I didn't see that," she said. "Now scat, cats."

I shook my head and stood up. "I call the bathroom first."

In the little space, I splashed water on my face and stared in the mirror. My eyes were red, and my throat was scratchy from all the cat dander in her apartment. At least she didn't smoke inside. That was against the building's rules. Not that Karen was usually the type to follow rules.

I didn't even bother running a brush through my hair—it would just create a fuzz ball. So I readjusted my ponytail and left the room to Jere.

Within thirty minutes, we were back on the road, and Karen was directing us to a gas station.

"You won't have me to rescue you this time," she joked from the back seat.

I'd offered to sit back there, but she declined. Said she wanted to put her feet up.

Jeremiah cringed.

We pulled up to a pump, and I slid down in my seat as Jeremiah filled the tank, trying to sleep even though I knew it would be impossible. Sixty-mile-an-hour wind and shuteye didn't exactly go together.

He drove away from the gas station, and Karen yelled, "Right! Turn right here!"

Jere slowed. "The interstate is this way."

"I know. I don't trust 'em."

I turned back to her. "The interstate?"

"Too many cops. And stupid drivers."

"Yeah, but it's faster," I said.

She shrugged. "Getting pulled over'd slow us down, I'd say."

"I'll take a different way," Jere said. "It's fine."

I faced forward and rolled my eyes. "Fine." I was just going to try and sleep anyway. They could figure it out.

Of course, I should have known Karen would be sleep's biggest inhibitor. If she wasn't talking, she was singing. If she wasn't singing, she was arguing with Jeremiah about his no-smoking rule. If she wasn't arguing, she was crunching on pistachios and throwing the shells out the side of the car.

Red lights flashed behind us.

"Are we getting pulled over?" I asked.

"Looks like it." Jere glanced in his mirror and turned his signal on to get on the shoulder.

"On a *highway?*" I asked, giving Karen a pointed stare.

CHAPTER 14

Meanwhile, she was sinking down in the seat, staring at her phone, doing her best to look invisible.

Two cops got out of the car and sauntered toward us. My heart pounded faster, and I gripped the door to steady myself. The last time I'd spoken to a police officer...

They were right beside us now, on either side of the car.

"License and registration," the one on Jere's side said.

"Yes, sir." He reached in the glove compartment and came back with the documents.

The cop scanned them, then looked at Karen and me.

"Ya'll think littering's fun, huh?"

"No, sir," Jeremiah said.

The second cop piped up. "Looks like there's room in here for your trash."

"Yes, sir," Jere answered.

"Then why," the first cop said, "are you throwing trash over the side of the vehicle?"

Jeremiah and I both turned to Karen, who had sunk so low in her seat, she was practically pint-sized.

"Don't look at me!" she yelled. "It was them. Damn kids!"

My mouth fell open. "Karen!"

The cops faced each other.

"That's enough," the first one said. He scribbled on his pad. "A warning." Then he handed the slip to Karen. "For the damn kids."

CHAPTER FIFTEEN

"You sellout!" I said when we were back on the road.

Jeremiah wore an amused smile. I could only imagine the laugh in his eyes, hiding behind his sunglasses.

"What?" Karen said. "They always go easier on kids! I'm not as cute as I used to be."

"You're ridiculous," I mumbled.

"What about it?" She stuck a cigarette in her lips, pulled out a lighter, and started flicking it.

"Hey!" Jere said.

She waved her arms and mumbled around the smoke. "Relax! There aren't even windows here." She finally got it to light, then sagged back in the seat. "Cops take it out of me." She took another drag and blew it out.

The smoke barely existed before the wind took it away.

"You need to turn up here," Karen instructed, but Jeremiah was already on the exit.

I looked between them. "How did you know where we were going?"

Jere fidgeted with the volume dial. "Lucky guess."

A sign for a ferry flew past us. "We're getting on a boat?"

"A ferry," Jere corrected.

My stomach curdled. Or rather, the gas station sausage sandwich Aunt Karen had gotten me did. "Can't we drive around?" I asked.

"This is the fastest way," Karen said. "I thought you were worried about the time? I have no idea why. Race isn't 'til Saturday. We could drive a couple hours a day if we wanted to. Take in the sights."

I shook my head. Not because I couldn't come up with a retort, but because Jere was pulling up to the gates, saying he wanted a stall on the boat, DRIVING onto the ship.

A million terrified thoughts raced through my

mind, not one of which I could vocalize. So I settled for white-knuckling the door. I leaned my head back against the seat, closing my eyes and trying my hardest to pretend I was anywhere but here. And failing.

I couldn't pretend forever.

"We have to go sit in the waiting area," Jere said.

"I'm fine here."

Karen was already up and out. "They have a smoking area at the front of the deck. See you back here."

Jere watched her leave and then whispered, "Can we start calling her Krazy Karen? Please?"

A bark of a laugh escaped my lips. "Whatever you want."

Was it possible to pass out from fear? If so, I might welcome it.

"Hey." Jere's voice was soft, as soft as his hand covering mine gripping the seatbelt. "It's okay to be scared, Syd."

I opened one eye and glared at him. "Oh, really? Figure that one out on your own?"

He smirked. "There she is, folks."

I shook my head and closed my eyes.

"Really," Jere said. "You need to get up on the deck of this boat."

"And why is that?" I asked, eyes still closed.

"Because," he said, "we need to find out if we can see another sunrise color for Liam."

I rolled my head to the side, looking at him. "You don't play fair."

He lifted his shoulders and turned his eyes upward with a little smile. "It's the truth."

"Fine." I unbuckled and got out of the car on shaky legs. Jere was already there to steady me.

His hand rested on my back, and I stepped away. We didn't need a repeat of what happened under the car. Or what almost happened.

I shook my head to clear the thoughts. "I'm fine. Let's go." I started walking away from the car.

"We need to go this way." He pointed in the opposite direction.

My cheeks heated as I turned around and headed the other way.

Together, we walked up the stairs. The higher we got, the more it seemed like the stairwell was closing in on me. When we finally reached the top, I held on to the guardrail and gulped fresh air.

"You're doing great," Jere said quietly.

I gave him a look, then took another step out. The ferry only rocked a little in the waves, but it was enough to make me feel like I needed to hold on to something. I made a few quick steps and fell into one of the seats on the main deck.

Much more gracefully, Jere sat down next to me. His eyes weren't on me or my lack of grace though. He was watching the sky. I followed his gaze and almost gasped. This sunrise was definitely a new color of orange. There were pinks and blues and streaks of yellow mixed in, too, but the orange was radiant.

I got my phone out of my pocket and snapped a few shots, but none of them compared to the sight before us. "I wish a picture would do it justice."

"We'll just have to remember it then."

CHAPTER SIXTEEN

Karen wanted to sit up front this time. She said we were too quiet. I told her she made enough noise for all of us.

"Oh hush," she said.

I sat back in the seat and smiled. Now it was light enough out—and dry enough—for me to work on the scrapbook for Liam. With my headphones in and music playing from my phone, I got a blank page and a pen and told him all about the sunrise, how beautiful it was, and that Jeremiah and I had watched the colors in the sky change together. Liam would have liked to know that.

I wrote about the time Greg and I were training for cross-country the summer before high school and how he used to get us up for runs at the crack of dawn. He always said the sunrise was its own reward.

I didn't agree with him them, but maybe I did now.

The sound of Jeremiah laughing caught my attention, and I wiggled out an earbud to hear them better.

Karen started talking. "When they were babies, they were inseparable. They had this little language they used to talk to each other. They would babble until they were blue in the face." She paused. "Those two weren't like regular siblings, you know with all the fighting and whatnot. They were more like friends."

Jeremiah nodded. "He loved her."

My lips trembled, and I looked down at my lap. I put the earbud back in my ear because I couldn't hear more about Greg and how much he had loved me. I'd failed him. Jeremiah and I both had. It wasn't something we could make up, get a redo on. We were stuck with our decision—and its consequences—forever. I couldn't imagine a day for as long as I lived not thinking of Greg or feeling the twist of guilt in my stomach at his loss. At my parents' tenuous marriage. It was all our fault, mine and Jeremiah's, just for a stupid kiss.

I sighed and settled back in the seat. I couldn't focus on writing now. My eyes were burning and my chest aching. I just needed to fall asleep for a little while and forget it all again.

I don't know how long I slept, but I blinked my eyes open to see a clear blue sky overhead. The Jeep was stopped, and a lot of cussing was coming from Aunt Karen.

"You know how to change a tire?" she asked.

Jere mumbled something noncommittal.

"What?" she asked. "They don't teach that in driver's ed anymore?" She swore again. "Guess it's time you learned." She raised her voice. "Sydney! Get out!"

I sat up. "What's going on?" I asked.

"Flat," Jere grunted.

Groggily, I got out of the vehicle and stood along the desolate highway, staring at the completely flat tire. It looked so sad compared to the rest of Jere's vehicle.

Aunt Karen had Jeremiah take out the spare tire and the jack, then she taught him to jack up the Jeep and take off the lug nuts. She was actually pretty good at teaching—aside from all the smoking and swearing.

Finally, Jeremiah had the tire off, and Aunt Karen was wheeling it over the ground, inspecting it. "Aha!" she cried and pointed at a spot in the tread. "There it is."

A nail head poked through the side of the tire.

"That's not good," she said. "They're gonna wanna sell you a new'n."

Jere shrugged and wiped his forehead. Money wasn't an issue for him.

"Pop quiz," Karen said. "How far can you drive on a donut?"

Jere's eyebrows came together. "A foot?"

"What do you mean?" I asked.

"I mean..." He looked between us. "You'd squish it, right?"

What he was saying hit me, and I broke out laughing. "Not the kind you eat. A spare tire is a donut!"

Karen grinned between us. "Cut him some slack," she said. "He doesn't have a papa like yours."

He didn't. For as absent as Dad had been the last few months, he used to be more involved.

He'd even taught me to change the oil in my car and rotate the tires.

The thought of my dad not going back to how he used to be—not being married to my mom—made my gut sink.

"I'm still waiting for the answer," Karen said.

"Fifty miles," I answered, just to put Jere out of his misery.

I took out my phone to look at the GPS. "There's a town about fifty miles from here," I said. "Ocean City."

Jere's eyes lit up. "I know the place."

CHAPTER SEVENTEEN

About an hour later, Jere pulled into a diner that looked like something out the '80s as if he'd been there a million times. Maybe he had.

"This doesn't look like a tire shop," I said.

"No, but I'm hungry," Jere said. "All this talk about donuts." He winked.

Karen laughed. She immediately got out and started smoking, but Jere turned and looked at me.

"You're going to love this place," he said.

I looked down at my clothes, all rumpled and covered in cat hair from sleeping on Karen's couch. "Should I change first?"

He gestured at the sign. "Does this look like

the kind of place where you have to worry about how you look?"

The faded spray paint sign that said "Bubby's" seemed to be in danger of rusting out and falling down at any minute.

"Come on." He took my hand and pulled.

Light sparked between our hands, and I backed away from the feeling.

"What?" he said.

"I..." At the hurt look in his eyes, guilt swept through me. "I'm going to get a sweater."

His shoulders seemed to relax as I went back to the trunk. It gave me just enough time to rub my hand, to discharge the electricity that had been there.

He held the door open for me, and I walked through.

"How do you know this place?" I asked. "Don't your parents make you eat at places that use, like, cloth napkins and two forks?"

He tapped his nose.

I'd hit the nail on the head. But he still didn't tell me how he knew about the restaurant. Or Ocean City for that matter.

We seated ourselves. There was barely a booth open in this space filled with families and couples and work friends and waitresses and mouth-watering smells.

Jeremiah slid into the booth and smiled across the table at me. "How could you not love a place like this?"

I didn't have an answer, so I reached over to pick up a menu sitting in a rack with condiments and sweeteners.

"Guess it's between Sally's Salad and Tilly's Tilapia," I said, quirking an eyebrow.

He grinned and picked up a menu. "You're telling me Bubby's Burger isn't an option?"

I snorted. "They should have named it Grammy's Sandy."

He laughed. "You just came up with that?"

A little self-conscious, I nodded.

"Not bad, Syd," he said, his eyes back on the menu. "Not bad."

"So what's the plan?" I asked. "Are we driving to New York today?"

"Did you want to get there tonight?"

I shrugged. "We don't have to be there 'til early Saturday to register."

"Good." He grinned and nodded his head toward the older woman walking toward us. "Because you're about to meet Plan B."

The woman reached the table, her eyes the same expressive brown as Jeremiah's. They screamed warmth and friendliness. "You didn't tell me you were coming to visit!" she cried, wrapping him in a hug so tight, I could feel the love from here.

Jeremiah squeezed her back. "I didn't know I was until about an hour ago."

She still held him to her chest as she turned to me. "Who's your friend?"

I smiled at the woman, even though every second I looked at her threw me off. Jeremiah resembled her so much.

"This is my friend Sydney," he said.

It could have been the flickering lightbulb overhead, but her eyes positively danced. "Sydney." She said my name like she'd heard it more than once before. Then she turned to Jere and whispered, "*The* Sydney? Greg's sister?"

Jeremiah's smooth skin turned pink as he tilted his head toward me. "*Bubby.*"

Her eyes crinkled even more at the corners. "I'll take that as a yes." Then she turned back to me. "I'm Bubby, Jeremiah's grandma. And this is my restaurant." She took my hand and squeezed. "Order anything you want."

CHAPTER 17

Karen walked into the restaurant and over to us. "Hi there," she said.

Bubby looked from her to us. "Another friend?"

Multiple appetizers, entrées, and chocolate shakes later, we all sat at the booth with Bubby and Hoolie, Jeremiah's grandpa. Everyone in his family seemed to have a nickname and eyes that told a million happy stories.

Plus, Bubby's food tasted like it was hand-delivered by the gods. She helped me take carb-loading to an entirely new level. Eventually, Hoolie left to help the waitstaff close down the restaurant, leaving Jeremiah and me alone with Karen and his grandma.

After we talked about school and college plans and Liam, Bubby asked us the question that seemed to be hanging over us since we arrived.

"You know I'm glad you all came," Bubby said, "but what are you doing here?"

I kept my lips on the milkshake straw, drinking slowly and deliberately to see how Jeremiah would answer this one. For once, Karen was silent, waiting for us.

He glanced at me. "We're going to the city, for the marathon."

"A marathon?" she repeated, shocked.

Jere nodded.

Bubby turned her gaze to me. "There's more here."

I stepped in. "My brother—he was going to run the marathon for Liam. And since he can't..." My throat got tight. I still hadn't gotten used to talking about Greg in the past tense—saying his name out loud.

Karen rubbed my back, and Jeremiah covered my hand with his. Instead of wanting to pull away, I wanted to lean into the warmth.

"I need to do this for him," I finished.

Aunt Karen wrapped her arm around me and squeezed.

Jeremiah nodded. "Me too."

I looked at him, then Karen, and said, "Thank you," before I even thought of the words. I wouldn't be here, in the restaurant, on the way to New York City, if it weren't for Jeremiah and Karen. No matter what our past was, I felt grateful now. And now was all we had.

CHAPTER EIGHTEEN

If Bubby was a house, her house would be it, warm and inviting. There were handknitted throws, framed needlepoints, and family photos everywhere. Plus, it smelled like vanilla and lemon.

She shrugged out of her jacket and hung it behind the door. "Would you like some cookies?"

"Of course," Jeremiah said at the same time I said, "No, thank you," and Karen said, "Yes, please."

"I should probably get some rest," I finished.

"Why don't you show Sydney the second guest bed, Jere?" Bubby said. "I'll be in the kitchen with Karen."

"Sure." He readjusted my bag over his shoulder.

"You don't have to carry that," I told him for the second time that day.

"I know."

He started down the hall, and I followed him, my feet sinking into the thick carpet. He turned right at the last door and opened it up. "She must think I really like you," he said. "This is always where the married couples get to stay."

I raised my eyebrows. What was that supposed to mean?

He set my bag down, then jumped onto the bed. The springs squealed underneath him. "Super comfy. But super loud. No one's doing anything in here." A Cheshire grin covered his face. "Come try it out."

I stood frozen. Jere and me in a bed?

But he patted the comforter.

So I walked to the bed and lay down beside him, leaving about a foot of space between us. I tried to focus on the popcorn ceiling with flecks of silver, but I couldn't because my body was hyperaware of Jeremiah. Of his arm so close to mine. Of the way his weight on the bed made me want to shift closer and closer to him until there was no space left.

"What do you think?" he asked.

I couldn't think. Not with everything that had happened today.

"Your grandma's nice," I said instead.

Jeremiah blew a little breath through his nose. I couldn't tell if it was a quiet laugh or a half-hearted sigh.

"She is," he said. Then he turned to look at me, and I turned to look at him, and now I wasn't looking at the ceiling, but diving headfirst into the most beautiful brown pools I'd ever seen in my life.

"It feels good having you here," he whispered.

I nodded, because I thought I understood what he meant. Like I knew more of him before he was Jeremiah at Sweet Water. This was his past. And it was lovely.

He reached out and gently moved a loose strand of hair off my cheek. "Goodnight, Syd."

"Goodnight."

The bed creaked loudly as he got up, like it didn't want him to leave either.

Jeremiah paused in the doorway and leaned

his head against the frame. "Let me know if you need anything?"

"Yeah."

Then the door closed, leaving me to myself and Jeremiah somewhere else. Separated, like we should be. But if that was how it should be, why did my chest ache more now than it did before he walked out?

I changed into my pajamas, which were way too warm since I'd been planning to sleep in my car. Still, I pulled the quilt all the way to my chin and breathed in the scents of Bubby's home.

These sheets hadn't been washed in a while. They were clean, but I could hardly smell the detergent.

Why hadn't Jeremiah's family come to visit her? Was it because of his dad's job?

I still remembered when Jere's family moved to Sweet Water because his dad had been transferred to be the senior vice president of a major resort.

We first met at the back-to-school barbecue our freshman year. I had accidentally bumped into him in line, and he jumped away.

"Ouch!" he'd yelled, his eyes wide and darting to his shoulder.

My stomach had dropped to my knees. "I'm sorry!" I cried. "Did I hurt you?"

He let out a long breath and wiped his forehead, relieved. "No, I was just worried your hair had burned me."

It took me a few seconds, but I got it.

And by that time, he and the few people around us who had heard him were laughing too.

My cheeks got hot, probably bright enough to match my hair. And I promptly left to avoid him and devise a plan to never see him again until graduation, when we'd surely go to different colleges on opposite sides of the country.

When I'd finally found Greg at one of the tables, he'd already loaded his plate full of hot dogs and hamburgers and cookies.

Greg used to hate how thin he was and that our parents forbid him from playing football because of it. Little did he know his long legs were perfect for cross-country. That he'd fill out with muscle and be one of the school's star runners.

"Greg," I'd said. "You have to hide me."

"Who is it this time?" he asked.

"I don't even know his name."

"Can you really hate someone if you don't know their name?"

I glared at him. "Hate's a strong word." But then I glanced around to make sure this guy wasn't coming anywhere near us. Maybe I did hate him. Just a little.

"That's fine," Greg said. "I have someone you can meet instead."

He ate a big mouthful of burger and stared across the cafeteria. How he managed to be so social with a Goliath-sized piece of food in his mouth, I had no idea.

Greg gulped down his bite and waved at *that* boy. The one with brown hair and wide eyes and a smile that promised a joke was coming soon. Probably at my expense. "Jere! You meet my twin?"

Suddenly, avoiding Jeremiah wasn't an option.

Not then, and certainly not now.

CHAPTER NINETEEN

Waking up to the sound of soft footsteps, hushed voices, and coffee brewing was a magic all its own. The Thane house had been silent since January. Coffee could be made at work. Conversation had stalled indefinitely.

But waking up in Bubby's house brought me back—back to a happier time in my life. Hints of coffee and breakfast reached my nose, and my eyes fluttered open to soft light coming through the curtains. Voices sounded, quiet and gentle, indistinct but kind.

I could have laid there forever, in the warm comfort of the bed, trying not to make the springs creak so no one would know I was cocooned here, enjoying the morning.

If Greg were here, he would have already been awake, in the kitchen, sneaking bits of food before it was ready and being everyone's best friend.

The thought brought a smile to my lips and revived the dull ache in my chest. I wondered when thinking of him would only bring a smile. If the ache would ever subside. In a way, I hoped it would, but the pain made me feel connected to him too.

It was too early in the morning for thoughts like that. I had to move—to get dressed and start my day and put my thoughts on the task at hand. Any task would do.

I checked my phone first. Mom had messaged me hours ago, around five in the morning.

Mom: How r u this morning?

I stared at the letters. Typing out the abbreviations had to be harder than letting her phone autocorrect to the whole word.

But that thought was just a distraction from another one.

How was I?

CHAPTER 19

Physically, I was fine—in better shape than ever before.

Mentally? I didn't even want to go there.

Sydney: I'm feeling better.

My stomach twisted with guilt. Mom had lost everything—her son and maybe her marriage. She had to be afraid of losing me too.

So I typed out a new text message.

Sydney: Hope you're having a good time with Dad. Love you, Mom.

For the millionth time, I wondered what would happen if she found out where I had been. If Liam's parents would ever tell her about how I ran the marathon for him. Would she be disappointed? Angry?

I decided, just like I always did when I thought this over, that I would take the risk. I needed to do this. For Liam. For Greg.

The light in the room had gone from soft to bright when I heard footsteps coming down the hallway. A few knocks sounded on the door.

I sat up and drew my knees to my chest under the blankets. "Come in," I said.

Jeremiah cracked the door open, peeked his head in. His gaze traveled from my eyes to my lips and back. "Breakfast is ready."

I nodded. "Be there in a second."

Why did breakfast sound like so much more than what I smelled from the kitchen?

I stood up and stopped asking myself those questions.

Those questions led me to places I didn't need to go. Hopes I didn't need to have. Fears that didn't need to be realized.

When I reached the kitchen, Jeremiah was the only one there. He sat at the table laden with eggs and biscuits and gravy and hand-canned jelly in every color.

"Where's Karen?" I asked.

"The restaurant with Bubby, and then they're going shopping." He stood up and went to the coffee pot. "You like coffee with cream and cinnamon, right?"

I didn't ask how he remembered that. Just nodded and went to the table, sat in one of the cushioned chairs covered with clear vinyl.

As I helped myself to a plate of eggs and biscuits, I asked, "Did you make this?"

"Yeah. Except the jelly. That's all Bubby and Hoolie." He set the cup in front of me, the steam lifting over the perfect mocha liquid.

I smiled. "Thank you," I said.

"Of course."

For a few minutes, the only sounds were muted chirps from outside and the scrapes of our silverware on the flowered dishes.

When all of our food was eaten and the dishes were in the sink, Jere smiled at me. "So," he said. "What do you say we go have an adventure of our own?"

CHAPTER TWENTY

First, he asked me how many miles I was supposed to run today.

When I told him four, his eyes lit up. "Perfect."

We got in his Jeep, and he drove me through his grandma's town, the little one his family used to visit for Thanksgiving, Christmas, and Easter. Ocean City, Maryland had a main street with boutique shops. A few motels. Some high-rise apartments. An insurance agency. And then Bubby's restaurant, which I could already tell was the heart of the town. At least, it was for me.

Somewhere between Bubby's and a bakery, the songs from our drive started cycling over again.

"Looks like we're at the end of your playlist," I said. "I'll pick the station this time."

I got out my phone to go to my music app, but he shook his head. "I don't have Bluetooth in this car."

I gaped at him. "You're telling me Jeremiah 'Fancy Pants' Dermot doesn't have Bluetooth in his car?"

Grinning, he shook his head. "My middle name is actually Devon. But close."

With his arm draped over the door and his shades reflecting the sky, he looked like he belonged here. Not in Ocean City, but in this moment, with that smile and the wind sifting through his hair with featherlight fingers.

"So you just listen to CDs?" I asked.

"Yep."

"I didn't even know they still made those."

He laughed. "Come on, they still make CDs. And this one is my favorite."

"Sure." I reached forward and hit eject on the player. "Time for something new."

"Wait, it's—"

The disc came out, and my eyes widened at the handwriting on the CD. My brother's.

I held it carefully in one hand, half ready to

cry and half ready to laugh. A mixture of the two escaped my lips.

I read the words out loud. "Greg's Groovy Mix."

Jeremiah looked at me and then the CD. "He didn't like my taste in music."

I shook my head. "Of course he didn't."

He laughed. "He made me that so we'd have something good to drive around to."

My eyes stayed on the silver disk. At his slanted scrawl in purple sharpie. He probably hijacked that marker from my room. It wouldn't have been the first time.

I traced my fingers over the letters, feeling closer to him and farther away than I ever had before.

"You can have it," Jeremiah offered. "If you want."

I shook my head and put it back in the slot. "No. This is where it belongs."

And for some reason, I felt that way too. Like I belonged here, in this car with Jeremiah. On one last adventure for Greg and Liam before life changed even more than it already had.

We listened to the music as we drove through town, but now it meant so much more. I let my hand hang out the window and felt the wind fly through my fingers, moving and shaping them at its whim.

The airstream slowed as Jeremiah turned and parked in front of a boardwalk that ran the length of the beach.

"Down this path and back is 4.7 miles." He got out and laid a hand on the hood to steady himself as he grabbed a foot and stretched.

I stepped out of the car, and he said something, but I couldn't focus on his words. He had his arm pulled across his chest, showing his muscles through the cut-off sleeves of his shirt.

How had his torso gotten so tan this early in the season? Had he been training on his own schedule before track try-outs? And when had he gotten a tattoo?

I couldn't quite read what the small print said.

And now I *really* couldn't, because he knew I was staring.

His eyes met mine, and he smiled a smile that was way too smug.

I turned my eyes down and tried to focus on stretching. Even though Jeremiah had admitted to watching me run past his house in the mornings, I still felt self-conscious. What did I look like next to him? He seemed so sure of his body, of how he existed in space. I'd gotten better, but I was still doing well to put one foot in front of the other without tripping or spraining an ankle.

My phone rang from the car, and I jogged back to it. "It's Mom."

He nodded.

I held the phone to my ear. "Hello?"

"Honey," she breathed. She sounded so nervous.

"Are you okay?" I asked.

Her deep breaths came through the receiver. "I was worried. I just woke up from a nap, and I had the worst dream." Her voice shook. "I should have come back the second I heard you were sick."

"Mom—"

"I'm just going to get a flight home. I probably can't get there tonight, but maybe by the morning—"

"Mom, Mom, Mom," I said, trying to slow her roll. "I'm fine. You just had a bad dream. And you need to be there for Dad, remember? For your marriage."

She let out a soft cry. "He doesn't need me. He doesn't even want me."

CHAPTER 20

I leaned against the car. My heart went out to her, and I didn't know how to help. Not from Ocean City. Not even when we were in the same house.

"Mom, he needs you. You need each other."

Jere looked at me, his eyes troubled. "Everything okay?" he mouthed.

I shook my head and looked down.

"I need my kids," she said.

We both knew that couldn't happen, but still, I said, "I'm right here. And I need you there." I bit my lip. "I need my parents."

Not the walking ghosts of them. The ones who moved around the house like the other didn't exist. I needed my parents. The mom who helped me find clothes that made me look like I actually had a figure. The dad who lived to play board games on Friday nights.

Mom took a few steadying breaths. "I'm here, baby."

My lips twitched. "Good."

A loud noise sounded across the beach, a group of girls in bikinis and guys in board shorts, screaming and singing like chimpanzees.

"What was that?" Mom asked.

"The TV," I said without pause. "You know how Karen likes her shows."

"Ugh."

"I know."

"Take care of yourself," Mom said. "Until I can. You have a steaming bowl of homemade chicken noodle with your name on it when I get home."

"Thanks, Mom."

"I love you."

"You too, honey," she said. "You're my everything."

I hit end and stared at the lock screen of my phone. A photo of Greg and me at the beach. I wished he was here. He could handle this. Could somehow lift up the sky, even when it was falling down.

I couldn't be Mom's everything. That was too much pressure. How could I get her to see that she needed Dad? That they could be each other's rock? I definitely couldn't be.

Jeremiah's hand covered mine, covered the screen. "Leave it in the car," Jeremiah said. "And stop worrying about everyone else. Life's too short."

That hit me. Hard. And I agreed with him. I

could have a day or a week or fifty years left, and it would never be enough not to live in this moment, not to feel the breeze coming off the waves or watch the way light danced in his eyes. I didn't want to miss a minute.

CHAPTER TWENTY-ONE

For a while, he stretched out, taking longer than necessary, and I appreciated the space he gave me. I needed it. But now I wanted to see the boardwalk moving beneath my feet. To get lost in the steady rhythm of heavy breathing and aching muscles and sweat dripping from my hairline down to my chin.

"You good to go?" I asked.

He nodded.

"Good," I said. "But I'm a little slower than you are."

He batted his hand like it was no big deal that he could run circles around me. "It'll be a nice, easy run. I just wanted to show you the boardwalk."

We started off slow, and eventually short conversation about our surroundings gave way to measured breaths and the pounding of our feet over wooden slats.

I might not have been a cross-country star like my brother or Jeremiah, but nothing cleared my mind like running did. This marathon could have been Greg's last present to me, the gift I needed to keep moving, keep putting one foot in front of the other.

Running next to Jeremiah felt as natural as the waves washing over the shore. Was this what it felt like for Greg and him when they trained together for cross-country? Like they were the two pillars on the pier, standing together but apart, working toward a common goal?

We were getting closer to the end of the boardwalk, but Jere veered off the path, and I followed him into thick sand that covered my ankles and leaked through my laces.

My legs worked to keep up with him until the shore came closer and he flopped down on the beach, breathing hard. I dropped beside him, and my chest rose and fell with his, our breathing growing steadier by the second.

He reached out a single fist, and I laughed at the gesture, tapped his knuckles with my own.

"You've gotten better," he said.

Something inside me swelled, heated. "Thanks."

"No problem." He sat up and rested his arms on his knees. A bead of sweat dripped from his hair, traced a path around his eyebrow and down to his jaw.

I reached out and brushed it away with my thumb. Heat through the liquid, shot straight to my chest, my heart.

The look in his eyes told me he felt it too.

I turned away from their depths and trained my gaze on the lovely, unfathomable deep of the ocean. Scary, beautiful. Just like these feelings taking hold in my core and refusing to let go.

"So what's on the agenda?" Jere asked.

I shrugged. "Nothing. Honestly, I was just going to camp out until the race. Are you sure your grandparents are alright with us staying here?"

"Are you kidding? They're thrilled."

"They're not going to tell your parents?"

He shook his head. "I'm not the only one with a chip on my shoulder."

Bubby holding a grudge hardly seemed possible, but then again, I barely knew her. So here was this perfect stranger offering us a place to stay. A warm bed and food for the next three days.

"That seems better than my plan," I admitted. "And I'm pretty sure Karen isn't a camping person."

He nudged me. "Is that a yes?"

I nudged him back. "Sure is."

He smiled and looked down, running his fingers through the sand. "So about tonight..."

"Yeah?"

His head tilted toward the pier and the small amusement park there. "Wanna go?"

Instead of no, another answer came to mind. "Why not?"

CHAPTER TWENTY-TWO

When we returned to Bubby's house, I took a shower. A long one that washed away the stress of the last two days. By time I got out, the house was empty, a note sitting on the kitchen table.

Went to help Bubby at the restaurant. Lunch is in the fridge. I'll come get you for supper. Call if you need anything. – J

I ran my hand over his "signature." I never understood why people only signed with one initial. It wasn't that hard to write a few extra letters. But I liked the way Jeremiah wrote his letter, messy, almost like an afterthought. I liked that he thought I would know who J was.

Because I did. I still had a few notes that he'd

passed me in class tucked away in binders. Dumb ones that said how lame the assignment was or asking if Greg would be free after practice. I'd kept them just for that signature.

It all seemed silly now.

If only I had the same worries that I had back then.

The distant sound of my ring tone hit my ears, and I hurried back to the bedroom to see who it was.

Liam's mom's name came on the screen.

My heart dropped. No. Please. Not now.

I swiped to answer, my fingers shaking. "Hello?"

"Syd?" Liam's voice came through the phone.

"Liam." Relief swept through me, so strong I sagged to the bed, making the springs protest loudly. "How are you?"

"Good," he said.

"How many colors now?"

"Three hundred and twenty-six."

I smiled. "Good. What's up?"

"I wanted to see how the trip was going. It's boring here."

I smirked. "Tell me Ms. Louisa didn't hear you."

"Of course not."

"Good. The trip is..." I sighed, thinking back to him and Jeremiah ambushing me. "Well, you'll be happy to hear who picked me up when my car broke down."

"Jeremiah?" Sometimes Liam sounded a thousand years old, but right then, his voice held all the earnest hope of a scheming ten-year-old.

"Jeremiah." I tried to keep the smile from my voice. And failed.

"No way!"

"Way."

"Yes!" he said. "You're talking to him, right? It would be a really boring trip if you weren't."

I scrunched the towel in my hair. "Why are you so invested in this?"

He was quiet for a second. "You and Jeremiah were Greg's favorite people. It doesn't seem right that you lost each other too."

My eyes turned down, and my hand stilled in my hair. We shouldn't have been Greg's favorite people. But I couldn't let that tear me apart, especially not with Liam on the phone. I nodded. "I think you're right."

"Of course I am," he said. There was some yelling in the background. If I didn't know him, his family, his situation, I would almost think it was just another normal kid on the other end of the phone.

"Oh, I better get going," he said. "Grandma just got here."

I smiled. "Have fun."

"I will. And don't be too hard on Jeremiah."

I crossed my fingers. "Promise."

"Uncross your fingers!" he said.

"How did you—"

"I just knew."

I laughed. "You're too smart for your own good. Have fun with your grandma."

"I will. Bye. Love you, Syd."

"Love you too, kid."

I lay back on the bed, still holding the phone to my ear. Relieved tears leaked out my eyes. Liam was still alright.

I curled up under the comforter and repeated that line in my mind until I fell asleep.

Liam was still alright.

For now.

CHAPTER TWENTY-THREE

*J*eremiah had texted me to let me know he was coming to pick me up for supper in an hour. Which would have been fine if his text hadn't said he was looking forward to seeing me. And if I wasn't looking forward to seeing him too.

I stared at my open suitcase, at the athletic wear and fleece pajamas, wishing I had packed something different and then hating myself for wishing that.

Going to eat and then the amusement park with Jeremiah wasn't a date—he hadn't called it that, at least—but still my heart had moved to the bottom of my throat, and it pounded furiously.

Running shorts might have been fine for the

boardwalk. Fleece pajamas worked for the married couples' bed. But for an evening with Jeremiah...

I sighed and reached into the bag, pulling out a gray jersey sweater and black leggings. That was what most girls wore anyway. And just to prove how much I didn't care about this non-date, I put my curls into a bun on top of my head and passed on makeup. Except mascara. I needed that.

For me.

Not Jeremiah.

Definitely not Jeremiah.

I sighed and stared at myself in the mirror. "Pull it together, Thane."

"What?" came Jere's voice.

I spun around, gripping my chest. "You scared me!"

Jere leaned against the bathroom door frame, laughing.

"Just for that," I said and bopped him with my mascara tube.

He clutched at the spot where I'd hit him on his shoulder. "I'm wounded."

"You're about to be if you don't stop smirking at me."

That just brought another laugh. "You couldn't be mean, even if you wanted to."

"Try me," I said, but I had to turn away, because I was already smiling. He was right. "Are you ready?" I asked.

He nodded, his hair falling perfectly over his forehead. My eyes followed his hair down to his lips, and I'd be lying if I said I didn't notice the way his shirt clung to him. How his faded jeans hugged his muscled legs. How did he look so perfect?

Right. He'd packed for spring break. Not whatever this was.

When I met his eyes, I realized he'd been watching me check him out. My cheeks heated, and I ducked past him. "Let's go."

I couldn't stand this. It had to be the married couples' bed. The off-limits-ness of it all. I needed to get outside and away from Jeremiah's cologne. From those brown eyes that said everything and nothing at the same time. Ignoring him had been easier from a distance.

We walked together to his Jeep, and he started to come toward the passenger side with me.

"What are you doing?" I asked.

"This." He opened the passenger door.

CHAPTER 23

I stared at his hand, then at him. "What is this?"

He shifted his eyes from me to the seat. "Whatever you want it to be."

"Nothing. It's nothing." I bit my lip and got in the car.

If it bothered him, he'd wiped the look from his expression before getting in on his side. We listened to Greg's mix on the way to the restaurant, and I kept my eyes on our surroundings. People were out and about. The girls I saw wore shorts and bikini tops for the most part. I was overdressed.

As far as I could tell, Jeremiah didn't notice them. His eyes never lingered on their bodies like most guys' did.

I liked that fact more than I should have.

Instead of turning into the restaurant's parking lot like I thought he would, he went a different direction and parked in an alley.

"Is this where—"

"I murder you?" he finished, wagging his eyebrows deviously.

I gave him a pointed look. "Well?"

He snorted. "No. Call your mom before she calls you and it's too loud to answer."

I lifted my eyebrows, and he tapped his forehead. He'd planned ahead.

Mom picked up the phone on the first ring. "Honey, how are you? Do you have a fever? Is your stomach alright?"

"I'm fine," I said. "Almost one hundred percent."

"Good," she said. "Good."

"How are you and Dad?"

"Great. This is a good place."

My brows furrowed. "When we talked earlier, it kind of sounded like—"

"You caught me at a weak moment." She brushed me off. "I needed a nap."

"Hadn't you just woken up from a nap?"

"I'm fine," she asserted.

"Mom, it's okay if you're having a hard ti—"

"I'm not," she said. "Tell me about your day. How's Karen?"

I sighed and looked at Jere, who was doing his best to pretend he wasn't listening. "She's fine. But I'm tired. Is it okay if I let you go?"

"Of course. Get to feeling better. I'll be home before you know it."

"Love you."

"You too, honey. More than air."

CHAPTER 23

I pulled my phone away and held it in my lap. In a few seconds, Mom ended the call.

Jere cleared his throat. "You know, if you're not up to going out tonight..."

I shook my head. "I am." I put my phone in my purse. "I am," I said again to convince myself. I hadn't agonized about spending time with Jere only to back down now.

His eyes caught mine, and he smiled like he knew how good it looked. "Let's go."

CHAPTER TWENTY-FOUR

Walking into Bubby's restaurant felt like coming home. I could see why Jere liked it so much.

But when I went to sit in an empty booth, he took my hand and kept walking.

My hand flamed in his, and I had the newly familiar sensation of wanting to pull apart but needing to get closer.

He walked me to the back of the restaurant and stopped at a door. "Are you ready for the private room?"

I lifted my eyebrows. "For..."

"Seven minutes of heaven."

My eyes widened, and he burst out laughing.

"It was a joke, Syd." He pushed the door open, revealing a simple room with big, round tables spread apart. One of them had a white tablecloth and flickering candles. Shells decorated its surface.

I looked from him to the table, in awe. "What is this?"

Hooking his thumbs in his pockets, he shrugged. "It was all Bubby."

Bubby's voice sounded behind us. "Are you just going to stand there, or are you going to sit down?"

I startled and turned to her. She carried a platter laden with seafood, and Hoolie and Karen trailed behind her.

"That looks delicious," I said.

She smiled. "Thanks, sweetie." She walked to the table and started setting out the food. "Did you and Miah have a good time today?"

It seemed like everyone was anxious to hear my answer.

I nodded. "It was good. I actually got a call from Liam." As Bubby set the table and we settled in, I told them about talking to him and how excited he was that Jere and I had gotten stuck together.

Karen chuckled. "Smart kid."

Jere nodded, and I shrugged. Liam's words were still running through my mind. *It doesn't seem right that you lost each other too.*

Hoolie said, "So what damage did you girls do out shopping?"

Bubby and Karen turned to each other and giggled. How were they so close already? Grinning, they started telling Hoolie about all their finds in the shops at the boardwalk.

Jere cut into his lobster. "What are you thinking about?" he whispered so only I could hear him.

I shrugged. "Nothing."

"Lies." He looked up at me, a challenging smile on his face.

Turning my head toward the short blue carpet, I shrugged again. Lying was easier than telling the truth.

But he waited for it.

So I said, "Liam. When I saw his mom's number on my phone, I really thought…" My throat tightened so much I couldn't get the words out. The unspeakable.

Jere put his hand on the table, palm up, and waited for me to rest my fingers in his.

I did, and chills ran through me. Most people talked about hands fitting perfectly together. Ours didn't. His hands were long, elegant. Mine were spindly, knobby, freckled. Just another reminder that we didn't belong together.

I tore my eyes from the contrast and met his.

"I'll be here for you," he said. "When it happens."

Because it would happen. We didn't have a say in that any more than we had a say in Greg's death.

The realization of what that thought meant flashed through my mind. I didn't have a say in Greg's death. There were things I could have done differently though.

Jere's fingers gently touched my chin and lifted it so I had to see his eyes, but he didn't speak right away. Just held me there.

Finally, he smiled a soft smile and said, "You have a million thoughts running through your mind, don't you, Sydney Thane?" He lowered his fingers. "Let them rest. For a night. You can always pick them up tomorrow."

A corner of my lips lifted, and I nodded.

"Good," he said.

When I tore away from him, I realized the

adults had been watching us. My cheeks warmed, and I became focused on my food. It was amazing, even with my stomach putting its tumbling skills on display.

"So," Bubby said, "Karen, Hoolie, and I have been talking about this trip."

Jere and I looked at each other. This couldn't be good.

"Yeah?" he said.

"We decided," Bubby said, "we want to come with you."

Jeremiah sputtered. "What?"

Bubby and Karen looked at each other.

"Well," Karen said, "your gramma and I hit it off today, and she wants to come watch our Sydney cross the finish line." She winked at me.

"I didn't know your brother well," Bubby said, "but I know how much he meant to my Miah. It would mean a lot if we could be there for you."

My eyes stung. There were so many people here to support me—support Greg and Liam.

Jere looked at me. "If it's okay with Sydney, it's okay with me."

I nodded, sending tears down my cheeks, and I wiped them. Bubby got up and squeezed me

CHAPTER 24

against her chest. It was like being surrounded by her love.

Karen got up and rubbed my arm. "We love you, honey."

I caught sight of Jere over Bubby's shoulder, and a line formed between his brows. His eyes were red. He fluttered his eyelids, blinking away the moisture.

"Love you too," I said.

When they pulled away, I watched Bubby press at the corners of her eyes with her thumbs. "Goodness."

She got busy clearing the tables. Hoolie gave my shoulder a squeeze, as well as Jere's, before helping Bubby with the dishes, and Karen followed them out.

For a moment, Jere and I sat in silence. I couldn't tell what was going through his mind, and mine had too much going on to even begin making sense of it.

Eventually, his eyes met mine. They were clear again.

"Are you ready?" he asked.

Jere didn't ask that question like other people did. The way he said the words made them sound like the evening was full of potential, not over.

Like instead of saying, are you ready to go, he was asking, are you ready to have the time of your life?

I said yes, because for the first time since January, I was.

CHAPTER TWENTY-FIVE

Jeremiah parked along the boardwalk, closer to the carnival. This time, we walked over the wooden slats, slow and leisurely. Just a few hours later, it seemed like an entirely different place.

Beach volleyball games and sun baking girls had given way to bonfires and music and gleeful shouts.

Even feet apart from the parties, I felt so distant from that life. Would that be me a year from now, in college? I couldn't imagine it.

A sharp breeze came off the waves, and I tightened my jacket around me, glad I'd opted for leggings instead of shorts.

"I forgot how cold it gets here at night," Jere said.

I nodded, even though I didn't have any memories to compare it to. Just home. Whatever that meant now.

When we got to the carnival, Jere paid my way in.

"You didn't have to do that," I said, even though I barely had any money of my own.

"I know."

For a couple minutes, we walked, not really heading any direction.

"Hey," Jere said, "have you ever seen someone making saltwater taffy?"

I shook my head. "I don't think so."

He took my hand and led me to a small shop. Through the glass windows, a man sat, spinning long strings of pink candy. Something about it was hypnotic and calming.

"Jeez," Jere said. "You'd think making candy would be a fun job."

"What do you mean?" I asked, my eyes still on the strip of taffy.

"He's mean mugging."

I turned my gaze on the guy whose expression

was so sour he could have flavored a whole batch, then spun around so he couldn't see me laughing.

The sound of Jere's laughter joined mine.

"Talk about RBF," I said.

"What's that?"

"Umm." My eyes darted around. "Really?"

"What?" He laughed.

I leaned over and whispered it in his ear.

He stiffened. "Yeah?"

I pulled back, tightening my jacket around me. "Welcome to the twenty-first century, Jeremiah Dermot."

He rolled his eyes. "Come on. That has to be colloquial."

"Colloquial?" I raised my eyebrows. "Didn't know I was in a vocabulary lesson."

His lips lifted in a smirk. "Whatever. Come on. Let's check out the rides."

"Which one should we go on?"

I followed his pointer finger to the tallest ride there. It had to be at least a hundred feet tall, with seats on each end. The thing slowly spun to a start, and soon the people were flying through the air in broad, sweeping circles.

"No," I said. "Absolutely not."

"Come on, Syd, it's fine. Five-year-olds go on that thing."

"Not me!" I cried. "I can barely get on a boat, and you want me to get on that...that...thing?"

"Yeah, unless you're too chicken."

He tucked his elbows back and made bawking sounds. Some people walking by laughed at him.

"Stop it, Jere. You're just embarrassing yourself."

He danced a chicken circle around me, still clucking.

"I'm not getting on."

"Fine." He stopped. "But then I guess you'll never know my secret."

I rolled my eyes. "I'm not falling for it."

"Fine," he repeated and started walking toward the ride. "It's a pretty good secret though," he called over his shoulder.

I stayed, feet planted. People passed around me in a flurry of excitement.

I grit my teeth together and jogged to follow him. When I reached his shoulder, I said, "Is there really a secret?"

His smile was way too satisfied. "Maybe. Get on the ride to find out."

CHAPTER TWENTY-SIX

The second the carnie who had two missing teeth strapped me into the contraption with oily sides and grimy seats, I knew I'd made a mistake.

I just didn't know how bad the mistake was until they spun us to the top.

My fingers dug into the bars over my chest, and I squeezed my eyes shut tighter than I ever had before.

"Hey," Jere said. "You can't see the view if you don't look down."

I shook my head. "This was stupid. Why did you let me do this?"

"You're the one who was so desperate to know the secret," he said.

I winked open one eye to see him, but immediately slammed it shut. Everything below us was so tiny. I could hardly even see the waves—they just looked like ripples in the ocean. "I'm going to be sick."

"You're going to have fun." Jere's hand covered mine, and he leaned his head forward. "In three, two, one..."

The ride swung down, and suddenly, my stomach, my body was weightless, flinging through the air on the arm of a metal machine, with only a harness and Jeremiah to hold on to. I screamed, clutching tighter to his hand than I had held onto anything else in my life.

His shouts were joyful. How could we be right beside each other, doing the same thing, and having two totally different experiences?

Somewhere between rounds three and four, the falling sensation in my stomach became the new normal, and I could watch the ground come up under us and then grow more and more distant without feeling like I was going to pass out.

Maybe that's what grief was like. You didn't lose the pain; you became used to it, lived with it.

The ride eventually slowed to a stop, and the guy let us out. "Have fun?"

"Oh yeah," Jere said, then looked at me.

My voice came out shaky. "I'll let you know in about five minutes."

He chuckled and walked off the platform with me. "You survived. How bad was that?"

"The ground's not spinning anymore," I said, "so that's good."

His laugh came again, and I fell for the sound. He was so carefree here.

"So what's the secret?" I asked. "It better be good."

Jere stalled and lifted a hand to my cheek. His thumb traced a slow path over my cheekbone. "Spending time with you is the happiest I've been since January."

My stomach tightened, and I looked toward the ground, barely able to form a simple, "Oh."

He didn't let me linger on the revelation, just took my hand and started walking. After a few minutes, he stopped at a stand and bought us some cotton candy. We strolled around the park for a while, picking fluff off the big tuft and taking in the sights. There were some middle school girls walking around, texting and laughing and putting on this show of how confident they were with their heavy eye makeup and choker necklaces.

I smiled at them. I missed that age, no matter how awkward it was. Anything was possible back then.

Jere followed my gaze. "What did you always want to do when you were twelve but your parents would never let you?"

"Get a tattoo," I answered without pause.

"What?" he laughed. "Of, like, a unicorn or something?"

I glared at him.

"What then?"

My cheeks heated. "It's just as embarrassing."

"What?" He started walking backward, watching me.

He almost collided with someone.

"Watch out!" I cried.

"Tell me," he said.

I turned my eyes toward the darkening sky. "It's a secret."

"I see what you're doing." His lips twitched into a devilish grin. "What if I said we could make a tattoo happen tonight?"

"I'd say maybe."

He pointed toward a shop a little farther away. "Saltwatr Tats."

"They can't even spell water!" I cried.

"Let's hope they get yours right then." He grinned.

My eyes latched on the shop. I still wanted a tattoo, but my parents would never say yes. Now, they might as well have been a million miles away. I was about to leave for college. Who knew what their future would hold? Or mine, for that matter. Right now, I wanted something I could be certain of.

I started walking toward the tattoo shop.

"Syd," he said, catching up. "I was just kidding! You don't have to get a tattoo."

"I want one."

"You're sure?"

I paused, my hand on the shop's door handle. "You have one."

He looked like he wanted to argue, but I watched his expression change as he gave in. "Okay. I'll make sure they spell yours right."

We walked into the shop, and a girl greeted us at the counter. She had tattooed stars winging out from her eyes. "Can I help you?"

"I'd like a tattoo."

She handed me a clipboard, and I stalled at one line on the yellow page. *You must be 18 to get a tattoo. Parental consent does not waive this law.*

My eyes widened as I showed the form to Jere.

He looked from me to the page. "Do you really want this?"

I nodded. Now that we were here, I couldn't imagine leaving without getting this tattoo.

"Okay. Get it filled out."

A few seconds later, he walked to the woman, and they began talking in hushed voices.

Eventually, he reached in his pocket and handed her some money. I still had a stunned look on my face when she walked up to me with a big smile and said, "Let's head on back."

CHAPTER TWENTY-SEVEN

*J*ere sat beside me on the Ferris wheel, watching the sights pass around us.

I held my wrist out and marveled at my new tattoo. The ink was so fresh, the black contrasted to my pale skin and made the perfect design. I'd asked for 26.2 mirrored to 26.2 with a heart in between.

"It's perfect," Jere said.

"I know." A sad smile touched my lips. "I wish Greg could have seen it." I looked at him. "You know?"

He swallowed hard, his eyes turning red again. "I know."

A cold gust swept around us, and I shivered,

even though I had my jacket on. Without hesitating, Jere put his arm around me and pulled me close. Being near him like this...it made me feel patched together somehow.

I leaned my head on his shoulder. "I miss him."

"Me too."

I tilted my head so I could see him, even while leaning on his shoulder. "Tell me about Greg?"

Jere waited for me to meet his eyes. "What do you want to know?"

"Everything."

So he did. Jeremiah told me about Greg, his best friend, not Greg, my brother.

The one who always had his back. Who refused to take part in drama. Who always wanted to have a good time. Who could be anybody's best friend but had chosen Jeremiah, the new kid, before he'd made friends and grown into his six-foot runner's body.

He said Greg loved me, protected me in ways I hadn't known or understood. There was a reason I didn't get picked on for my bright red hair or freckles that grew so thick in the summer I almost had a tan. A reason why guys didn't ask me out.

"No one was good enough for you," Jeremiah said. "I finally talked him into letting me ask you to prom. So you wouldn't have to go alone." He gave a wistful smile to the sand. "There might have been more to it than that. At least on my end."

I raised my eyebrows. "What do you mean?"

His eyes hit mine, held me. "You had to have known."

I waited.

"Come on, Syd," Jere said. "You know there was a reason we always hung out at your house. Why we always asked you to tag along. Why I had to kiss you on New Year's Eve." He shook his head. "Greg loved you, but I did too."

My mouth went slack. "You..."

He took my hands in his, pulled them close to his chest. "There's not anyone out there like you, Syd. You're smart and driven, and I know at any given moment there are at least a million thoughts running through your mind, none of them about you. How could I see someone like that, spend time with someone like that, and not love them? Not want more?"

I tried to speak, but my throat was dry. How could I respond to that? To the fact that my brother's best friend had been so much more than that, but always outside my reality?

The Ferris wheel stopped, and we got off.

Jeremiah took my hand, held it. "Come with me?"

I nodded, unable to find my words.

We crossed the wooden planks, veering off the boardwalk, and onto a secluded part of the beach. I could still hear music coming from the carnival, but it was faded.

We walked along the water, close enough to feel the salt in the air, far enough to keep our feet dry.

The black ocean looked like it could swallow us whole, if only we got close enough.

Jeremiah wasn't going to say it, but I was going to. No matter how *good* it felt to have my hand in his, he had to know how this would end.

"Do you ever think that we could be us again?" I asked.

"We are us," he said. "What else could we be?"

"No, Jere. That's not what I meant." I dropped his hand and tucked a loose hair behind my ear only to have it fly out again a second later.

"I mean us. Not damaged, not guilty, not anything but Sydney and Jeremiah."

"We are Sydney and Jeremiah." He took my hand again. "All of that stuff, it's part of us, but..." He cast his gaze over the water like he could fish for words there. "It's part of us, but it isn't us." He took my face in his hands. "You are more than your loss."

A stinging feeling hit my throat, and tears fell from my eyes, sliding down my face and landing on his hands. He brushed the streams away with his thumbs.

"Do you mean it?" I asked.

He nodded.

And before I could stop myself with reason or logic, I let my heart take control. My lips met his in a flurry of fear and sadness and tears and everything I'd felt since January. Everything I'd felt before.

His fingers worked their way into my hair, behind the ponytail, holding my face close to his. I held on to his shoulders, his hair. Every part of him needed to be close to every part of me. I wanted to forget where I began and he ended. He kissed me back with an urgency that told me he felt the same way.

He pulled me down to the sand, and I lay on his chest, savoring each kiss as it changed from frantic to feeling, rushed to relaxed, needing to wanting.

I pulled back for a second and gazed in his eyes, which looked dark black but held all the light in the world, then rested on his chest.

Sometimes you just needed someone to help you remember who you are. When you're minutes from falling apart and so lost not even a map could help you find your way back to yourself. You need them to remind you, because if they didn't, everything could just fall apart.

Right now, we were held together by the same invisible thread. I just hoped it wasn't close to breaking.

CHAPTER TWENTY-EIGHT

I could have stayed rooted to that spot, exploring Jeremiah's kiss, all night, but it was too cold to stay this close to the ocean breeze.

"Let's start walking back?" I asked.

He hugged me close, kissing the top of my head. "Okay."

Coming out of his embrace was like leaving the comfort of my bed on a cold winter morning. But he held me to his side, and that heat radiated through my body. I wrapped both my arms around his middle and walked through the sand with him, back to the boardwalk, back to reality.

We didn't speak for a while, just reveling in this, us, and what it all meant.

My eyes caught a cute storefront with seashells and peppermints hanging in the window. The sign said The Beachy Barista.

Jeremiah followed my gaze and kissed the top of my head. "Come on."

"What's in there?"

"You have to try an Ocean City hot chocolate."

He pushed the door, and it chimed open, revealing a room full of two-person tables with votive candles flickering in big seashells. The little lights danced in Jeremiah's eyes, making them come alive even more.

We sat at a table near the window, and Jeremiah scooted his chair so we wouldn't have to sit far apart, so we were both looking past the window display and into the lit-up boardwalk scene.

A waitress came and took our order over the dull chatter. Soon, we were sipping the sweetest cups of hot chocolate, filled to the brim with steaming liquid and topped with melting whipped cream.

I took a deep sip, letting it warm my body from the inside out.

Jeremiah looked at me over the top of his cup. "Good, right?"

I nodded.

He took a sip, leaving a puff of whipped cream on his nose. He was the world's best-looking mess.

"Why are you looking at me like that?" he asked.

"You have a little..." I pointed at my nose.

"Oh." He leaned in closer. "Something on my nose?" His eyes crossed like he was trying to see it, and I laughed.

"I can't see it," he said, eyes still crossed.

"You're ridiculous." I laughed.

He leaned in even closer, and soon, he was rubbing his nose against mine, kissing my cheek, and I didn't even care how silly it looked or that I'd soon be a sticky mess, because I was laughing so hard. A pure, tinkling sound coming out of my mouth that I hadn't heard in months.

"I think you have a little bit..." He gestured at his whole face.

I rolled my eyes and picked up a napkin. It scratched over my skin as I wiped away the mess, and Jere's eyes followed its every movement.

"There's a little more..." He leaned forward

again, and his lips found a spot right on my jaw, sending tingles down my spine.

Just like my wrist still burned from my tattoo, he might as well have tattooed that spot and called it his. Because I wanted it to be his, for the rest of this trip and after.

As we sipped the rest of our cocoa, I tried to pretend that things would never be different between us than they were in this moment, in the warmth of the coffee shop and our laughter.

CHAPTER TWENTY-NINE

We left the shop, hand in hand. I clung to him, wishing this night could last forever. I wanted to know more of him and this place that helped shape him growing up.

"Show me something else?" I asked.

"Sure." He led us farther down the boardwalk, away from the carnival, to a shop called Odds and Ends.

Through the stuffed window display, I could tell the shelves were packed from floor to ceiling with exactly that—odds and ends of every kind.

"Is it a thrift store?" I asked.

"Kind of."

My brows came together. "How can something be kind-of a thrift shop?"

"Come on." He tugged my hand. "You'll see."

Aside from the clanging, rusty bell hanging over the door, this store was much quieter than the last. An older lady behind the counter, sitting between stacks of books, told us to ask her if we needed anything. Jere promised we would.

He lowered his voice. "She's been here forever. She knows where everything is."

We walked past a shelf stacked with drooping succulents and another one covered in T-shirts that had faded Ocean City designs printed on them. As we got closer to the outer walls of the little shop, I realized full bookshelves lined every bit of the store. I hadn't noticed them with all the clutter. Someone could have spent an entire day exploring here and not had time to read even the titles.

"Here," Jeremiah said.

He stood in front of shelves of jewelry ranging from antique to gaudy to touristy.

I reached out and touched one necklace made of blown glass with an orange design inside. Watching the glass-blowers at the beach in Sweet Water was always a fun way to pass a few minutes.

Jere held something up. A delicate necklace

with a tiny, silver tennis shoe dangling from the end. "What do you think?"

I brought the charm closer and looked at it. "It's beautiful." Then I noticed the price tag attached to the chain. "But it's too much." It would have cost the rest of the cash I brought with me and then some.

"Good." He started walking toward the front of the store. "I'm getting it for you."

"Why?" I asked.

He nodded toward my wrist. "You have something to remember your brother. I want you to have something to remember me too."

As he left to pay, I stood there, my heart dancing jauntily. Remember him? What did that mean?

Was this just one night to him? Would we go back to Bubby's, back to Sweet Water, and pretend none of this had happened? I didn't want the only proof of this night to be a tattoo and a necklace. He'd already tattooed my heart and labeled it his.

He came back with the necklace unclasped, and I let him clip it around my neck. The charm rested on my chest, heavier than it should have felt.

We walked out of the store together, and I asked him, "What time is it?"

"Late."

"How late?"

He shrugged. "I don't have my phone to check, but they didn't give us a curfew."

"We should probably get back," I said.

He frowned but nodded. "Wait." He took my face in his hands and pulled me in close for a kiss. This one felt different. Like my good dream was shifting to a nightmare before I even really got to experience it.

After he pulled apart, he searched my eyes. "We're good, right?"

I managed a smile. "I hope so."

We walked to the car, hand in hand. And when we got in and got our phones, I realized how right I'd been. The dream was over.

CHAPTER THIRTY

Karen: Your mom called. Wants to talk to you.

Mom: Call me when u can OK?

One missed call from Mom.

Karen: Said you're in the bathroom.

One missed call from Mom.

Mom: I thought u were feeling better? Do u need 2 go 2 the hospital?

Karen: I told her you're not up to talking.

One missed call from Mom.
One missed call from Dad.

Mom: Honey, plz, just call me back. I'm rly worried.

Karen: She says she's worried.

Mom: If u dnt pick up ur phone Im calling 911.

Karen: I don't think I can stall her much longer.

Dad: Call your mom.

Mom: Im calling 911.

One missed call from Mom.

Mom: I rly am...

Karen: I had to tell them the truth. I'm sorry.

Mom: We r getting on a plane right now. Come home.

Mom: Y did u go 2 NY after we told u no?

Mom: Our flight lands @ 8. If u want 2 have a room when u get back, u better b home when we get there.

CHAPTER THIRTY-ONE

Jeremiah's phone had only two text messages on it. No phone calls.

Mom: Why are you charging your card in Ocean City?

Mom: We shut down your credit card. If you want us to sign your permission slip for track, be home tomorrow morning.

CHAPTER THIRTY-TWO

*J*eremiah and I sat in his car, parked by the boardwalk, immobile.

Even with still bodies, the same question ran through our minds.

What now?

CHAPTER THIRTY-THREE

*J*eremiah called his mom, but she didn't answer, just texted him and told him to find his own way home, to live with the consequences of his actions.

"I need to call my mom," I said. "Maybe she'll understand."

Jeremiah nodded, even though his expression was unreadable.

With shaking hands, I got to Mom's contact card and tapped call. It only rang once before she answered.

"Sydney Margaret Thane, you had us so worried about you!"

"Mom, I'm sorry, I—"

"After all we've been through, you skip your

senior trip, pretend to be sick, get your aunt to lie for you, and drive halfway up the coast with some boy. What the *hell* are you doing in Ocean City?"

"I couldn't—"

"You know what was going through my mind? I thought you'd died! I thought you had been kidnapped! I thought you'd run away! Do you know how that made your father and me feel?" Her voice rose with each word until she was shouting. "WE'VE BEEN TRHOUGH ENOUGH ALREADY! CAN'T YOU UNDERSTAND THAT?"

I held the phone away from my ear and blinked back tears. "I was trying to do it for Greg!"

"No, you weren't. You were doing it for yourself," she spat. "You wanted to spend a rule-free week with Jeremiah Dermot."

My stomach soured. "That is not even close to true."

"So you haven't kissed him."

Even though I'd been lying about everything, I couldn't lie about this. About him.

Her scoff was drowned out by an announcement made over a PA speaker.

"Mom, are you at the airport?"

"Where do you think we are?" she asked. "Of course we have to come back. You obviously can't be on your own."

Lead formed deep in my core. I'd hoped her texts were only empty threats. "You're not staying at the retreat?"

"No." Her voice faltered, and a sob came through the phone.

"Mom, are you okay?"

"No, I'm not okay. My daughter ran off, my husband wants a divorce, and my son is *dead*."

"Mom, I—"

"Save it," she said. "There's nothing you could say to ever make this better. Nothing."

The line went silent, and I stared at my blinking screen signaling the call had ended. I knew Jeremiah was watching me, but I couldn't face him. My throat burned like I'd swallowed fire. This couldn't be happening. It couldn't be happening. My parents couldn't be getting a divorce. Not after twenty years of marriage. Not after everything we'd been through.

Frantically, I dialed my dad's number and called him. His phone rang longer. So long I thought it might go to voicemail.

Eventually, his voice came across the line. "Sydney."

"Dad, what's going on?"

"I could ask you the same thing."

"Mom says you're coming home. That you want a divorce."

He let out a heavy sigh. "You're just a kid. You wouldn't understand."

"I'm not 'just a kid,'" I said. "I'm a senior. I'm about to go to college. I know enough to know this is a mistake."

"Well, unfortunately the deal is that you don't get a say in our marriage and what we do with it."

Tears streamed from my eyes now, unstoppable in force and number. My parents had been together for twenty-four years. Since they were freshmen in college. How could they be ending that now?

"Dad, I know I messed up, but what can I do? How can I fix this? There has to be something," I sobbed. "Please."

"No one can fix this." The even, careless way he said the words made me feel like I'd been slapped. "And I wouldn't want anyone to. It's over, Sydney, do you get that?"

"Do you really care that little about Mom?... About me?"

"That's not what this is about."

"Then what is it about?" Anger leaked through my voice. "Tell me."

"We'll talk about this when we get home. Goodbye, Sydney."

"No, I want to talk about it—"

My phone beeped at me.

The call had ended.

It was over.

CHAPTER THIRTY-FOUR

Jeremiah looked at me, waiting for answers.

I didn't have any.

After a long pause, he reached out and touched my shoulder. "Are you okay?"

I scoffed, shrugged my shoulder away from his touch. "Does it look like I'm okay?"

"No, but—"

I shook my head.

"Syd, I—"

I shook my head again. This was too much. I couldn't handle it.

"What do you want me to do?"

"So it's my choice now?" I turned my eyes on him.

"Hasn't it always been?"

"What is that supposed to mean?"

He raised his hands defensively. "It doesn't mean anything bad, it's just..." He reached out to touch my hands. "I've always wanted to make you happy. I'd do anything."

His fingers covered mine, but instead of marveling at them, I felt sickened by them and what they stood for. I pulled my hands back.

"You want to go home, don't you?" I asked. Accused.

"What choice do we have?"

I gaped at him. What choice did we have? "We could run the race, to honor Greg and Liam and what they wanted to do with their lives. To hell with our parents. We're graduating in May!"

"No," he said. "If I don't run track this spring, I might not get my college scholarship, and if I don't have a scholarship and my parents aren't helping me, I have nothing."

My jaw jutted out. "Except your dignity."

"Why are you turning this on me?" he asked. "You wouldn't be here without me. Greg never would have asked me to give this up."

"You're right," I said. "I wouldn't be here without you because Greg would still be alive."

Jeremiah's eyes hardened. "What are you saying, Sydney?"

"You know exactly what I'm saying."

His jaw worked back and forth. "I'm not the one who got in the car when I was drunk."

"He never would have done that if we had been around," I said.

"It doesn't matter," he spat back. "Greg knew not to drive when he was drinking. There was no reason for him to. There were other people around. *He* got behind the wheel. *He* drove away from the party. *He* crashed the car, and there's nothing you or I could do to stop him, if not then, than any other time."

I blinked back tears. "That's a cop-out."

"No," he said. "What's a cop-out is blaming yourself for his death and walking in a dead man's shoes. When are you going to admit that you are using his death as an excuse to keep from living your own life?"

My hand connected with his cheek so hard the slap echoed around us.

He stared at me, shocked.

I sat back in my seat and buckled up. I urged myself not to cry. Not in front of Jeremiah.

A couple of seconds later, the car shifted into gear.

We needed to leave, but I would never be able to get far enough away from him.

CHAPTER THIRTY-FIVE

I sat with my knees pulled tight to my chest as we drove in silence to his grandparents' house. In the last year, I'd caused my brother's death, ended my parents' marriage, fell for the completely wrong guy, and now I couldn't even finish the one thing Greg cared most about in his life: running this marathon for Liam.

Liam. Add that to the list of people I'd disappointed. I couldn't run the marathon for him. I was a failure, in every sense of the word.

I bit back yet another sob so Jeremiah wouldn't see me break down.

When we got back, Bubby, Hoolie, and Karen were waiting for us in the kitchen. I could see their silhouettes framed through the window curtain. As soon as we walked in the door, they greeted us with various versions of concerns and questions.

Jeremiah tried to answer them as they came, but I couldn't take another minute of his political responses.

"ENOUGH," I yelled, and everyone stared at me. "It's over. We just need to go."

Karen's eyebrows met on her forehead, and her eyes shone with concern. They looked too much like my mother's. "Oh, honey. It can't be over. Just give your parents some time to cool down."

"Jeremiah and I broke the rules, and now we're paying for it," I snapped. "Let's not make it harder than it already is."

"They're just scared," Karen said. "They'll come around."

"Come around from their divorce? You know this week wasn't just a vacation for them, right? They went on a counseling retreat, and now they're leaving early because of me."

Bubby covered her mouth with her hand, but her pity only fueled my fire.

"This was a dumb idea to begin with," I said.

"And if we don't get back, I'll lose a place to live and Jeremiah's parents won't let him run track."

Bubby gasped. "They wouldn't."

He looked up at her, nodded, then sagged onto the nearest chair. "I don't even know how to get back. Mom cancelled my credit cards. I'm nothing without my track scholarship, without my parents."

Bubby rushed to him and rubbed his shoulder, like this was the real tragedy.

I looked down to blink away my blurring vision. Karen must have known not to comfort me, because she stood feet away, studying the ground.

"We can pay for your gas," Bubby said.

Jere spoke to the carpet. "Thanks."

I looked at the pathetic guy sitting on his grandma's couch. I didn't know what I'd ever seen in him. He'd been a part in every terrible thing in my life. I was stupid to think he and I could have ever been us.

"I'm going to get my stuff," I said and went to the guest room.

After a moment, a knock sounded on the door frame. Jeremiah stood there, looking lost. "Sydney, is this what you want?"

"What, back to pour some salt in the wound?"

"Is this what you want?" he repeated with more force.

"Of course it's not what I want," I cried. "Do you think I wanted this?" I waved my arms around the room. "I wanted to go to the marathon, run the race for Greg, but you ruined that too!"

"I didn't mean to."

"But it happened," I said. "And I need to stop being dumb enough to think you're ever going to do anything but ruin my life."

His eyes turned red, and moisture filled his lashes. He sniffed and looked away. "Is that how you feel?"

I drew up the rest of my energy and put all of it into one word. "Yes."

"Be in the car in five. I'm going to get my bag."

After the door shut behind him, I slammed each piece of clothing into the bag with all the anger I felt in my body. I hated this. Hated that everything had come crumbling down. All because I was stupid enough to say yes to a road trip with Jeremiah Dermot.

CHAPTER THIRTY-SIX

*B*ubby and Hoolie told us to drive to the gas station near their house so they could fill up the Jeep and get some cash from the ATM.

Karen, the traitor, rode with them on the way, leaving Jeremiah and me alone in the Jeep again. Not a single word passed between us.

He drove up to a pump, and I got out. I needed space from him and the harsh words that had passed between us in that very vehicle.

Bubby and Hoolie parked at the next pump over. When Bubby got out of the car, she said, "Come on, Sydney. Let's go get some snacks."

She didn't say it in the sweet grandma way,

but in the Jedi-mind-trick way. *You will come inside and get snacks with me.*

When we got inside, I turned and eyed the junk food. This was exactly the kind of thing I'd passed on for four months because I'd had a marathon to train for... but now? Nothing. I could eat whatever I wanted.

The thought brought me no joy.

Bubby walked down the aisle, putting treats in my arms and muttering to herself about the snacks. She was trying to remember what Jeremiah liked.

My heart hurt for her. I hoped, for her sake, that Jeremiah would make an effort to visit them again after this trip.

"Anything chocolate is a winner," I said, hating that I knew him so well.

We stopped in front of the stand with rolling hot dogs and taquitos in oil-soaked paper bags. Pass.

"Can you think of anything else you need?" Bubby asked.

I shook my head.

"Okay."

I started toward the cash register so I could

unload my laden arms, but Bubby put a soft hand on my shoulder. "Sydney, hold on."

I turned toward her, ready for a lecture on the red mark I left on Jeremiah's cheek or the tears in his eyes, but she wrapped me in a hug. I couldn't return it with everything I was holding, but her warmth still seeped into me, cocooning me.

I stepped back. If she held me any longer, I'd fall apart.

"If I may..." She sighed. "I've been around the block long enough to know what love looks like, and when I see my grandson look at you..." She put her lips together and shook her head. "You know, the first time his family came to visit after they moved to Sweet Water, he told me about you and Greg and that he almost lost his chance with you because he made a joke about your hair. Even then I could see it in his eyes."

My own eyes stung, but I did my best to keep my mask in place. I trained my gaze on something right over her shoulder. A sign that said the slushy machine had broken down with imperfect spelling.

"I don't know what happened tonight between the two of you, but please, don't let it ruin something that is so special."

Bubby didn't get it, though. You couldn't ruin something that wasn't real. We were in a bubble here in Ocean City. And now that bubble had burst.

I nodded anyway because I couldn't take any more of her soft voice and words that were far too hopeful.

She put her hand on my back as we walked to the register, and even though I offered to pay, she got out her credit card and took care of it. She was used to taking care of people.

We went out to the Jeep together. Jeremiah already sat in the driver's seat, and Hoolie and Karen leaned against the hood of his grandparents' car, talking, laughing. Or, more like Karen was talking and Hoolie was laughing.

"I need a goodbye, young lady," Bubby said to Karen, sticking her arms out.

Karen got up and wrapped Bubby in a tight hug. They rocked back and forth like long-lost best friends.

How had Karen gotten so close with them already?

I guessed I understood. Jere's grandparents were great people. How could you not fall in love with them? My heart ached as I realized I was losing them too.

I changed directions and got in the back seat of the Jeep, bringing the snacks with me. Jeremiah didn't even look at me, his eyes straight ahead. Fine. I stared ahead too. In two hours, I could ask Aunt Karen to drive me home, and in three months, I would make sure to go anywhere Jeremiah wasn't. I wouldn't have to see Jeremiah Dermot ever again.

Karen's phone rang in the front passenger seat, but she was so preoccupied with Bubby and Hoolie, she didn't hear it.

It said "Moto Group" so I leaned forward and answered it. "Karen's phone."

"Hi there, we were just calling to see where we needed to send her last check. Do you know if she's still living at the same address?"

"Last check?"

"Yes," the guy said. "From the Motorcycle Group."

I caught sight of Karen, laughing and smiling with Jeremiah's grandparents. This was why she was able to take a week off at a moment's notice. "She's still at the same address."

"Thanks." The receiver bumped against

something and then the man on the other end said, "Tell her again how sorry we are. Times are just tough." the line went silent. I hurried to put her phone back in her seat and then sat back again. Jeremiah barely even gave me a second glance.

After they finished their goodbyes, Karen came over and got in the Jeep.

Hoolie leaned over the driver's side door. "Y'all have a safe trip, you hear?"

"We will," Jeremiah said.

"Good. And when you get home, I need you"—he pointed at Aunt Karen—"to stay in touch. I need you"—he pointed at me—"to take care of yourself. You always have a place to come stay with us." And then he pointed at Jeremiah. "And, Miah, I need you to make things right with this young lady. She's one in a million, and you'd be an idiot to let her go."

Jeremiah stared straight ahead, put the Jeep in drive, and said, "Goodbye, Grandpa."

CHAPTER THIRTY-SEVEN

We drove through the night to Aunt Karen's apartment in silence, not even listening to Greg's mix CD. I huddled under Bubby's quilt in the back seat. Karen put on her eye mask, leaned her head back, and smoked. And Jere? He might as well have been made of stone for all the emotion he showed.

Our sophomore year, he'd broken his ankle on a cross-country course, and it took him out for the season. Right now felt like that time all over again, with him withdrawing into himself. Back then, he'd disappeared for a few months, only going to school and home while he did PT. Like he was punishing himself for being in pain.

He didn't realize that he was punishing more

than just himself, though. We missed spending time with him. His sisters were worried sick, the oldest even made a weekend trip home from her first semester of college in California to make sure he was alright.

His withdrawal had deeply bothered me then. I couldn't understand why he would pull away from his friends at the worst time in his life. But Greg said everyone dealt with disappointment differently and that Jere'd be back when he was ready.

Greg was forgiving like that. Me? I still hadn't mastered that skill. The bitterest part of me was glad he was hurting and keeping his distance. I couldn't wait to get away from Jere—go back to the plan I had when I first met him freshman year and avoid him for the rest of my life.

How had he said those things to me? It was like Greg's funeral all over again. We'd been in the church my family only attended on Christmas and Easter, and I sat in the corner of the children's cry room before the service. I couldn't be close to the coffin, to the shell of my other half, knowing he was moments from being lowered into the ground. The whole ordeal made me feel seconds away from throwing up or passing out or both.

There, in the cry room, I could sit in silence while my parents talked to the pastor, try to be somewhere else, in my mind if not my body.

Jeremiah had found me there, sat across from me. "Are you okay?"

I'd scoffed. "Okay?" The only thing more ridiculous than his question was his timing. Gearing up for a day of people telling me it was in God's plan for my brother to die or that I could turn his loss into a message, I couldn't take one more thoughtless comment.

"I just meant..." He fiddled with his hands over his crossed legs. "Will you be?"

"No." How could I be? My lips twisted into a grimace. "It was our fault."

"How could you say that?"

"Are you kidding?" I stared at him, incredulous. "How can you be so dense?"

A muscle in his jaw twitched. "You know, you're not the only one hurting."

"Because of us."

He shook his head. "That's not fair to say."

"It wasn't fair that he died."

Jeremiah pressed up from the carpet. "You need some time. Let me know what I can do to help."

CHAPTER 37

"You know what would help?" I'd gotten up too, stared him right in the eyes so he'd know how serious I was being. "Stay away from me."

I'd left the room, Jeremiah, with every intention of following through on my own request. I didn't want to see him again. But now, here we were, pulling into the parking lot of Karen's apartment. I was wide awake, disappointed, and couldn't stand the idea of three more hours in the car with him. Taking a road trip with my enemy had been my worst idea, and I wasn't going to repeat it twice.

"Karen, can you drive me home?" I asked.

Her wide eyes went from me to Jere. "Are you sure?"

I nodded.

She faltered. "Well... sure." And then she carried her stuff inside.

I went to follow her, but Jeremiah called, "Sydney, wait."

I turned to face him, holding my hands out at my sides. "What?"

"Don't do this," he said. "Please."

Because we both knew what it meant if I rode home with Karen. It meant we'd go back to being worse than strangers, passing in the hall like trains on opposite tracks. Following through on what I'd asked him to do after Greg's funeral.

But that was how it had to be.

"You know when you said I had a million thoughts going through my mind?" I said. "What you didn't know was that in those million thoughts, your name was always there. I never wanted to be just Greg's twin sister to you. I wanted to be Sydney. To be something more. I wanted you to see *me*.

"But that was before I learned promises could be broken. That you were the kind of guy who would let his friend leave a party. No matter what you say, a piece of me will always believe there was more you could have done. You could have taken the keys before you took me outside, thrown them in the ocean. Hid the car. Anything."

But he hadn't. I hadn't. We hadn't.

And that meant I couldn't.

I couldn't give my heart to Jeremiah Dermot because it had been buried with my brother. And there was no way to get it back.

I shook my head. All I could say to Jeremiah now was, "Go home, Jere."

His lips wavered, but only for a second before his eyes were back on the apartment building and a tear was rolling down his face, blending with the saltwater already there.

"I'm sorry," he said.

And then he turned around and started to the car.

As I made my own trip into Karen's place, I wished. That things were different. That we could be more. That we could go back to the days when I was Greg's sister, and Jeremiah was the new guy.

But most of all? I wished Jeremiah hadn't been right about everything.

CHAPTER THIRTY-EIGHT

Even though we'd driven until two in the morning the night before, Karen was up at five with her travel mug and visor, ready to drive me home.

I pushed up from the couch and rubbed my swollen eyes.

"Are you sure you want to go home?" she asked.

I nodded. "What other choice do I have?"

"Oh, honey, we always have a choice." She sat next to me on the couch, and she was so light, the cushion barely dipped at all. "You have a choice to beg forgiveness instead of askin' permission. You have a choice to chase after that boy. You have a choice to forgive."

CHAPTER 38

"I've already tried all of those things, and look where I ended up."

"Hey, my place isn't that bad."

I laughed a little despite myself. "You know what I meant."

"I know." She leaned her head against mine and rubbed my back. "Okay, let's hit the road, Jack."

"My name's Sydney." I tried the joke, but it fell flat coming through my lips.

As she stood up, she shook her head, smiling. "Come on, girl."

After she said goodbye to her cats, we walked outside and down to her car in the parking lot. It might have been rusty, and one of the windows might have fallen down in the track, but I loved it. Anything was better than that Jeep that only played my brother's music and never gave me any respite from the rain or Jeremiah.

I got into her car, sitting on the pillow that covered exposed springs, and held my backpack on my lap. Somehow, I managed to fall into an uneasy sleep, but an hour in to the drive, my ringing phone woke me up.

I didn't recognize the number, but I answered anyway. "Hello?"

"Is this Sydney Thane?" a man asked.

"Yes?"

"We're calling to let you know we have your car impounded on our lot."

"What does that mean?" I asked.

"We had to tow it off the freeway," he said matter-of-factly. "It'll be twelve hundred dollars to get it out. You can come get it when you're ready."

"I...I don't have twelve hundred dollars."

"I guess you'll get your steps in then."

With wide eyes, I rested my phone in my lap.

"What happened?" Karen asked.

"My car...was impounded."

She shook her head, a wry smile on her lips. "Welcome to the hard knock life, kid."

Welcome? I'd already built a house and lived there. More like home sweet home.

CHAPTER THIRTY-NINE

I wanted to sleep more—knew I needed it, but as we wound our way down obscure highways, I couldn't relax enough to actually disappear in slumber. Instead, I got out the scrapbook I had been making for Liam.

The decorated cover stared back at me, mocking me, just like my new tattoo. Now, it would only be a reminder of another way I'd failed Greg. Maybe I deserved that. I shouldn't be allowed to forget and move on, because Greg couldn't.

"Is that Liam?" Karen asked, nodding at the cover.

"Yeah," I said. I'd placed a photo of him and

Greg together right in the middle. They looked so cute, grinning together and wearing matching Halloween costumes. Greg would have made an amazing dad, but he would never have the chance. Liam wouldn't either. And now he'd never be able to have a marathon medal to hang around his neck.

"He looks sweet," Karen commented.

"He is."

I stared out the window, where a pastel orange sunrise painted the sky. Why had I never noticed all the colors of sunrise before Liam? He seemed to catch the little things everyone else missed. Maybe because he knew they could be gone any minute. He had to savor every single moment.

Was it better to know your time was short so you could appreciate it more? Or had Greg been the lucky one to be here one second and gone the next, never worried about death or what he'd leave behind? *Who* he'd leave behind?

I flipped to the last page of the scrapbook, where I'd written silvery letters to spell MARATHON. There was no photo to put there now. Only an excuse.

I got out a pen and started writing.

Liam, I messed up. I made a promise I couldn't keep,

and now you're going to suffer for it. Sometimes, you learn that no matter how much you want to do something or help someone, it just doesn't work out. You get kicked down. Your parents tell you no. You get a flat tire or a speeding ticket or run out of gas. You try to mix oil and water. I know you wanted Jeremiah and me to have each other, but we're bad for one another. Greg was our glue, and without him...it just doesn't work. I know how much you wanted this and how much Greg wanted this, but I couldn't make it happen. I hope you understand, even just a little bit. I hope you know that I love you and that I tried my best. You deserved better.

I dropped the pen, unable to write any more through the blurring in my eyes and the fiery lump in my throat.

Couldn't that last line sum up his life? He deserved better. He deserved better than terminal cancer, than losing his best friend in my brother, than all the suffering he'd experienced in his short life.

And I was just piling on.

I hated myself even more for that. Hated my parents for making us turn around. Hated Jeremiah for giving up. Hated myself for giving up.

The thought of disappointing Liam ripped my chest to shreds.

"Are you okay, honey?" Karen asked.

There was that question again.

I shook my head, sending a tear flinging off my nose. I wiped at the itching sensation.

"Let's stop," she said. "Get some fresh air."

She pulled off the road into a turnoff for a field. There was a barbed-wire gate with a big black sign that read NO TRESSPASSING in bright orange letters.

The engine quieted, and she opened her creaking door.

"Get out," she said.

I shook my head, but her glare told me if I didn't get out, she'd drag me out herself.

My body felt like a million lead balloons, but I dragged myself out of the car and sat on the hood. It was warmer here than it had been in Ocean City, and the morning sun heated my skin from the light and from the hot metal hood.

"Take a breath," she said.

I did and caught a whiff of her cigarette. "Can I have a pull?"

She eyed me. "Did you just say 'a pull'?"

"Come on." I stuck out my hand. "If there was ever a moment to smoke, this is it."

Something about my demeanor must have

CHAPTER 39

told her I needed this, because she handed it to me and said, "Don't inhale."

"Fine." I took the thin filter end between my fingers. It felt foreign, dangerous, forbidden—different from anything I'd experienced. Carefully, I held it to my lips and sucked. Acrid smoke filled every crevice of my mouth.

I opened wide and watched the smoke lift in the air while a strange sensation spread everywhere the smoke had been.

This time, I wanted to be braver. Freer. Everything more than I'd been before.

I held the cigarette to my lips again, and this time I breathed it in, wanting this *different* feeling to spread throughout my body and replace everything I felt now.

And it did spread, like poison.

"Sydney!" Karen yelled, yanking the cigarette from my hand. "I told you not to inhale!"

Coughs racked my body so hard I had to sit up. My eyes watered—from the pain or from the coughing or from the smoke, I didn't know.

While my coughing eased, Karen rubbed the butt of the cigarette on her rusted hood, leaving a trail of black ashes.

She patted my back. "Take it from me, Syd, runnin' from your feelin's never does you any good." She nodded her head toward the car. "You good?"

I was anything but.

CHAPTER FORTY

I told Karen I needed to use the bathroom at the next gas station when all I really needed to do was get this taste out of my mouth. How she smoked one cigarette after another day after day, I didn't know. It made me wonder what pain she was hiding from.

She stopped at a gas station in a town so small I wondered if it was even on a map. I stood in the parking lot for a second, taking in the towering grain elevators and the empty street. Maybe I belonged in a town like this, or better yet, in the middle of the country where I couldn't hurt or disappoint anyone.

I sighed and started inside. This store smelled like it was eighty years old and used to allow smoking. Maybe my body was just more in-tune to that now.

The bathroom here was only a room with a toilet and a sink, no stalls. Thankful for the privacy, I locked myself in and started the water running in the sink as hot as I could get it. Which, unfortunately, was only lukewarm.

I stuck my mouth under the stream, letting it wash over my lips and tongue. Even after a minute of that, I could still taste smoke. It stuck to my skin, just like my pain. Another layer of the new me that I couldn't seem to shake no matter how hard I tried. Maybe I deserved it for being so stupid.

I used the toilet, washed up, and bought some gum before going outside. Karen stood beside the pumps, talking on her phone.

As I got closer, I heard her say. "Sydney's coming my way. I'll talk to you later."

She tapped the screen and put her phone in her pocket. "Ready?"

"Yeah." I dropped into the seat on my side of the car. "Who was that?"

"Your mom." She laced her fingers on top of the steering wheel and looked at me. "I want to tell you something, just so you'll be ready."

CHAPTER 40

My heart clenched, and my mind went to the time I learned that Greg had died in an accident. Jeremiah and I were still at the party. The cops drove up with my dad in the back seat, his face a mask for a mind that had already checked out.

I watched through a crack in the basement window curtains as the cop let Dad out of the car and they walked together toward the house. They knocked on the door, asking for me.

Something was wrong. Everyone at the party was still hiding because they'd been drinking underage, but Jeremiah stayed by me, walked beside me up the stairs as my legs shook.

They stepped inside and eyed us the way that adults eye kids who have been drinking. Dad just stood there, silent.

The cop looked at him. "Do you want to tell her, sir?"

His head twisted slowly, one side to another.

With a frown, the cop turned to me and said in a husky voice, "Honey, your brother was in an accident. He didn't make it."

I didn't know how Jeremiah reacted, but I shook my head, faster and faster. It couldn't be. I'd just seen Greg. He had to be at the party still. Playing video games in a bedroom. Hanging out with some girl. Playing beer pong in the garage. He hadn't driven away. Hadn't left us. Hadn't died.

"I know it's a lot to take in."

"Where is he?" I heard the words like someone else had said them.

Jeremiah. He'd asked them.

"They're taking him to the morgue. It was instant."

My first thought was why did people always say that like it was a consolation? And my second thought was that Greg was supposed to help me move furniture around in my room the next day. Why had that gone through my mind?

Maybe I hadn't loved Greg. If I had, I would have stuck with him. Would have been immediately devastated, not thinking about myself and how heavy my stupid dresser was.

"Sydney?" Karen put a hand on my shoulder, dragging me out of my past. "Your parents are sleeping in separate beds."

It shouldn't have surprised me, but it did.

"Oh," I said, my voice small. Of course they were sleeping in different beds. They were getting a divorce.

"Your dad is sleeping in Greg's room," she said. Another blow.

But sometimes, you got hit by so much, you started wondering what could come next, not how terrible the latest news was.

Karen waited for a moment, and when I didn't say anything, she put the car into drive and started away from the sleepy town. It looked a little sadder than before.

CHAPTER FORTY-ONE

As we got closer to Sweet Water, Karen asked, "Anywhere you wanna stop before we get home and you go into lockdown?"

A corner of my mouth lifted against my volition. She had a point.

My first thought was the hospice house. Liam. I had to tell him, give him the scrapbook, no matter how hard it would be to face him.

Like I'd said in my letter, he deserved better.

"Mom won't lock me out if we're late?"

Karen shook her head. "You give her too much credit sometimes."

I didn't know what that meant. "Would you mind driving downtown?"

Karen swallowed. But she nodded.

CHAPTER 41

"Liam's hospice is along the Riverwalk. Let me call and make sure it's okay for me to stop by."

"Go ahead," Karen said.

Even though wind roared in through her window and I wanted to do anything other than let Liam know what a failure I'd been compared to my brother, I dialed his mom's number. She'd be at the hospice house for breakfast.

It rang several times, but eventually her voice came over the phone.

"Hey," I said, trying to sound happy, even though I was crumbling inside. "I was just calling to talk to Liam."

Silence met me on the phone until she said, "Sydney, Liam died last night."

CHAPTER FORTY-TWO

*S*ometimes, when you know bad news is coming, you prepare yourself. You think you know how you'll react. How it will feel.

But every time, you're wrong. Nothing could have prepared me to hear those words come through the speaker.

The phone slipped out of my hand, and I covered my mouth.

No.

My cell landed on my lap, slid down my leg, and clattered to the floor. As I bent to pick it up, the only part of my body I could feel was my fingertips as they scraped little pebbles on the carpeted floormat.

My hand clenched around the phone, and I

held it up to my ear. "Hello?" I said again, wishing more than anything Liam's mom would have something different to say. I couldn't go home to nothing. No Jeremiah. No brother. No family. No Liam.

"Sydney?" her voice rasped. She'd been crying.

"Is..." My voice failed.

"The funeral is Friday at ten. I know you'll be in New York." She paused. "He would have wanted you there."

"I'm...sorry," I managed.

"I am too," she said.

The call ended, and I barely kept myself together long enough to dial another number. Jeremiah. No matter what we'd been through in the last twenty-four hours, he deserved to know.

"What's going on?" Karen asked.

But I couldn't tell her without falling apart.

"Yes?" he answered.

I didn't know what I'd been expecting, but it wasn't the indifferent tone he gave me.

"Have you heard?"

"About what?"

"Liam."

"No."

"He—"

"*No.*"

"—died," I finished. The words cut up my tongue, made my entire mouth burn.

Karen gasped beside me.

The line was quiet.

"Jere?"

"I'm here."

I didn't know what to say, so I waited.

"I'll talk to you later."

"That's it?"

"There's nothing else to say," he said.

The call ended, leaving me alone in the car with Karen and my grief. Suddenly, that sadness seemed like more than a part of me. It was me. It was outside of me. Sitting on my chest and crushing me whole. I couldn't breathe.

"Sydney, are you okay?" Karen asked, her voice sharp.

"Pull over!" I cried.

She swerved to the tiny shoulder of the highway, and I stumbled out of the car, falling into the ditch and getting covered in mud on my way down.

I gulped down every breath I could, but my lungs stung, and I cried out. I cried out for everything that I'd lost in this life. But mostly I cried out for the life that Liam and Greg had missed out on. The life I couldn't give back to them, no matter how much I wanted to.

Karen rushed around to me and surrounded me in her arms.

Why did things like this happen to kids? To innocent people who did nothing but good? Spread nothing but love? "Why?" I sobbed. "It doesn't make sense!"

She rubbed her forehead against mine, and her smoky breath poured over me. But right now, it was the only thing I could feel aside from the pain ripping my chest apart. "There isn't a reason," Karen said. "It just happens."

"That's not good enough," I cried. "It's not right."

"It isn't. No one deserves pain more than anyone else, but it exists. It's our job to survive it. To show it that no matter how hard it presses down on us, we can still get up." She rubbed the side of my face and stared at me, hard, willing me to do exactly that.

The problem was, I didn't know how I'd ever be able to get up again. Or if I even deserved to.

CHAPTER FORTY-THREE

Karen stopped at a truck stop and paid for me to take a shower.

As the water poured over me, I couldn't help but wonder what my life had come to. How I'd gone from the shy girl living in her brother's shadow to someone who snuck out of the house to drive halfway across the country. Who illegally got a tattoo and let herself fall for her enemy.

Whoever I was before, that perfect daughter, was only a shell now. I didn't know who I was on the inside.

I held on to the handle and twisted off the water, letting droplets make their way down my forehead, down my back. Each tiny bead fell and twisted away from me. Another layer gone.

CHAPTER 43

In less than three months, I'd be graduated from high school, moving out. My parents would be divorced. What would be left for me in Sweet Water? What would be left *of* me?

I squatted down and pressed my forehead to my knees, letting the short hairs there press into my skin. Another spark of feeling I hadn't had before.

I rubbed my fingers over my neck, and they caught on something. A necklace chain. Unlatching it with my unsteady hand proved challenging, but eventually I held it in a pile in my palm.

How could something look so different in less than twelve hours?

What used to be a sign of the best evening had turned into a reminder that everything had an ending, and not a happy one.

I took the white towel a couple quarters had rented us and scratched it over myself until my skin shined red. I wanted every layer of the old me gone. I wanted to be rid of the Sydney who ran off with Jeremiah for kisses so there would be room for someone new—anyone new—to exist in my skin.

I got dressed in the leggings and athletic shirt

I'd planned to wear during the marathon. Hours of research had gone into the outfit to prevent blisters and burns, but now it seemed immaterial.

Once I finished dressing and put my socks and shoes on, I walked back outside. Karen sat on the hood of her car with her legs crossed and a cigarette dangling from her lip.

On the way to the car, I tossed my muddy clothes and the necklace in a trashcan. No point hanging on to those either.

Karen barely hid the sadness in her visage as she put out her cigarette. "I'm gonna grab a snack. Want anything?"

I shook my head and went to the passenger side. Once I had the door shut behind me, I leaned my head against the head rest and closed my eyes.

After a few minutes, Karen's door creaked open, then shut, but the engine didn't start. "I can't stand seeing you like this."

"Then look away."

CHAPTER FORTY-FOUR

I kept my eyes closed until we started driving into Sweet Water. Traffic was worse here, and Karen didn't have the option to take obscure roads to our house. Every few seconds, she cursed under her breath. Her fingers were white on the steering wheel, and her lips formed a tight ring around her cigarette.

"Do you want me to drive?" I asked.

"No," she snapped, sending smoke out her mouth.

Fine then. I sat back in my seat and held on to the handle above my door. The closer we got to our house, the more feelings of pain and regret grew in my chest. If they got any worse, I might explode.

As she drove her car into the driveway, next to Dad's freshly washed and waxed convertible, I thought exploding might be preferable to going inside.

Her chest rose and fell several times as she gulped in fresh air. I could practically see the tension leaving her body.

"You ready?" she asked.

I shook my head but opened the door. I didn't have a choice.

Before we reached the front door, it was already open, and Mom was coming outside, wrapping me in a hug.

"I'm so glad you're alright," she cried. She reached out to Karen and held her hand. "I'm going to talk to you later."

Karen threw her hands up in the air and stormed inside. "I got her here, didn't I?"

Mom shook her head and took me in her arms again. "You're alright."

I pushed away from her. "I'm not."

Part of me was glad I couldn't see her face as I walked up the stairs to my room, past the empty spaces on the wall where Greg's pictures used to be, and lay in my bed.

She might have lost her son, but I lost my

brother and a friend who was like a little brother to me. And I'd failed them both. She'd never know how that felt.

I stared at the glow-in-the-dark stars on my ceiling. They used to bring me so much comfort. Now they just reminded me of a past I desperately wanted to return to.

Yelling seeped through the cracks in my door from downstairs. Karen and Mom had entered into one of their screaming matches. There was slamming and breaking. And then crying. And then nothing.

They'd made up. They fought like that every time we'd gotten together. But they always made up.

My door cracked open, and I expected to see Mom, but Karen peeked her head in. "Hey, sweetie."

"Hey."

She came and sat on the edge of my bed.

"Sounds like you survived the crusades," I said.

She snorted. "Your mother and I learned from the best. Grandma was quite the lady." She laughed to herself and rested a hand on my leg. "Your mom loves you, you know that?"

I didn't respond.

"That doesn't mean she's perfect."

That was the understatement of the century.

"I'm going to sleep downstairs on the couch tonight, for moral support." She squeezed my leg again and stood up. "You let me know if you need anything."

I nodded.

After the door shut, I went back to staring at the glow-in-the-dark stars until the actual sky turned dark outside and I couldn't stay awake anymore.

CHAPTER FORTY-FIVE

*M*om forced me to go downstairs and eat breakfast with them.

I'd expected to be sitting with her and Karen, but when I saw my dad at the end of the table, I froze.

"What are you doing here?"

He kept his focus on the waffle in front of him. "That's one way to greet your father."

I turned around to go upstairs. I'd starve before I sat at the same table with him.

"You wait right there," he barked. "Sit down."

"Or what, you'll leave me?"

He pushed against the table to get up, but Mom stood between us. "Please eat breakfast with us." She lowered her voice and her eyes caught mine. "Please?"

I ground my teeth together, about to tell her no, but then Karen met my gaze. The tilt of her chin echoed what she'd told me yesterday. *Your mom loves you.*

Wordlessly, I took an empty chair, and it was like the first bomb had been diffused.

On to round two.

Mom put a waffle on my plate and sat down in her own chair.

"Can you pass the butter?" I asked.

Mom held out the butter dish, but when I reached for it, she dropped it. The ceramic bounced on the table and shattered on the tile floor.

I gasped and went to pick it up, but she took hold of my hand and twisted.

"What is this?" she snapped.

"What are you—" Then I saw what she was staring at. My tattoo.

I tried pulling my hand back, but couldn't with the vice grip she was keeping on me.

"It's a tattoo," I said.

"I can tell." Her voice was icy.

Karen piped up, "It's cute, don't you think?"

Mom turned her glare on her sister. How Karen didn't disintegrate into a pile of ash, I didn't know.

"Did you have something to do with this?" Mom asked.

My aunt held her hands up, defensively. "Absolutely not. But as far as tattoos go, it's not like it's a pirate skull or a boy's name or…" Karen's voice quieted to a whisper. "Right, I'm going to the bathroom."

Dad, that coward, stood up too. "That's my cue."

But Mom wasn't ready to let him leave. "You stay right here. We are talking about this." She shook my hand in the air.

I used that moment to twist out of her grasp.

With a sigh, Dad folded his arms over his chest. "What do you want me to do about it?"

Mom looked at me. "She needs to get it removed."

Dad shook his head. "Are you coming up with two grand?"

"We *are* selling the house."

"Well, then, you can take it out of your half."

"My half?" Mom's voice rose. "She's half yours, too!"

They were talking about me like I wasn't even there. They might as well have just taken my photos down from the wall, too, and called it a day.

"I didn't tell her to get that tattoo," Dad retorted.

"And you think I did?"

"It's a damn heart and a few numbers. She wants to wear long sleeves to work the rest of her adult life, that's fine."

Mom rounded on me. "You're grounded. You're not leaving your room until you move out."

I glared at her. "You're the one who forced me to come down here in the first place!"

Dad started past us, bowl in hand. "Told you to leave her up there to pout."

My mouth fell open, and I left the room. I hated them like I'd only ever hated Jeremiah. The problem was I didn't hate any of them as much as I hated myself.

CHAPTER FORTY-SIX

*L*iam's funeral was scheduled for Friday morning, and Mom broke her grounded-for-life rule so I could go. Dad stayed at home, but Mom and I went with Karen, who'd gotten a neighbor to feed her cats and stayed an extra night.

The entire way to the church, questions I shouldn't have been thinking ran through my mind. Would Jeremiah be there? What would he think when he saw me?

Guilt coursed through me. Today was a ten-year-old's funeral, and all I could think about was a boy?

I needed to stop, and fast.

This church was on the other side of town,

farther away from the coast. Out here, the houses were spread out, the roadsides less decorated for tourists. It seemed realer somehow.

We drove up to the church where cars filled the parking lot and spilled alongside the street, parked next to the sidewalks. The building was small compared to the one where we had Greg's funeral, but just as crowded.

The three of us walked what seemed like half a mile to the church doors, and we found seats in the very back. Aunt Karen sat between us, holding Mom's hand.

Even though we'd never been here before, this place brought up memories for all of us. I'd known it would. I just didn't know how hard it would be to see the small coffin at the front of the church with flowers and a framed photo of Liam. His last school picture, before chemo made him lose his hair.

His blue eyes shined just as bright before his illness as they had with the sunrise reflected in them.

I tore my gaze off the picture; I had to if I wanted to keep it together. But that had been a bad idea. My eyes landed on none other than

Jeremiah Dermot, looking painfully good in a charcoal suit.

His entire face looked like the moon covered in clouds. Dimmed, a soft halo of what it should have been.

The pastor started the service, and I faced forward again. Unlike funerals for older people, no one ever had anything really comforting to say when someone young died. They could say the person was in heaven, that they would be with God and all the family they missed.

If you weren't religious, none of that was of any comfort. If you were, there was nothing that could be said about all the things they would miss in life. Greg and Liam would never go away to college, have a career, meet the love of their life, walk across the graduation stage.

We cried bitter tears along with the rest of the congregation, laughed at the funny stories, listened to the songs. But eventually, the pastor opened the microphone.

"If you have any stories you want to tell about Liam, how he impacted you in his short time here on Earth, the floor is yours."

For a little while, no one went. His grandma

tried to say something but was overwhelmed with tears. And then Jeremiah walked to the pulpit.

At the microphone, he cleared his throat, cast his eyes downward. Even from here, I could see the pain there.

"Some of you might know, but my best friend used to spend quite a bit of time at the hospice house with Liam. At first, I thought it was just something that kept him from doing homework with me or training for cross-country. But then my friend died.

"In the days after his funeral, I got to thinking about Liam. What he was going through and what my friend had told me about him. And I thought, he should still have someone come to visit him.

"I spent almost every Saturday afternoon with Liam. At first, we talked about Greg. A lot. I think he helped me grieve my best friend. Maybe because we were grieving together. But then I learned all of the awesome things about Liam. Like the pastor mentioned earlier, he watched every single sunrise, just to see how many colors of orange there were. You couldn't argue with him because he was just too smart. He loved

CHAPTER 46

Nurse Louisa's chocolate chip pancakes. And he loved my best friend's sister.

"You see, I wasn't the only one who thought of Liam after Greg died. My best friend's sister went to see him every Saturday morning before her run."

My heart stalled, but my muscles leapt to action. I tried to stand, to leave, but Karen held on to my hand.

"Wait," she whispered.

"Well," Jeremiah said, "eventually, Liam caught on. I was in love with my best friend's sister. And you know what he did? That sneaky little guy made a plan for us to meet and talk.

"You know what I learned from Liam? I learned that you can't let life or sadness stop you. You have to be brave enough to live and love through pain."

Jeremiah put the microphone back in the stand and left the stage.

CHAPTER FORTY-SEVEN

Only family was invited to the graveside service, so they had a quick reception at the front of the church so everyone could say their goodbyes, give their condolences.

The room buzzed with low murmurs and soft words. Slowly, the crowd worked its way into a disorganized line to see the family.

I remembered being in that line when Greg died. Everyone told me that we would push through those sad feelings. That soon we would remember the happy memories more than the sad ones. It had been four months, and I was still waiting.

Even with all I'd been through, I drew a blank

when Mom, Aunt Karen, and I reached Liam's mom.

"Sydney, what are you doing here?" she asked. "I thought you were going to New York."

My mom stiffened beside me.

"I was," I said. My lips trembled. "I disappointed him."

"Oh, Sydney." Liam's mom pulled me into an embrace and stroked my hair.

As I broke down into sobs, she whispered into my ear. "You never could have disappointed him. You were there for him. You loved him. He loved you."

"But if I loved him, I wouldn't have let him down," I cried.

"No, sweetie. You did what love does. You showed up when it mattered most."

She held me until I could stand on my own two legs, and I nodded, wiping my eyes. "I'm so sorry." For your loss. For not running the race. "For everything."

She reached out and brushed her fingers over my wet cheeks. "Thank you. For everything."

I let the crowd push me away, and I stood off to the edge while Mom and Karen said their regards.

Mom reached into her purse and wrote something on a scrap of paper, handed it to Liam's mom. They hugged for almost as long as we had.

As the three of us walked out of the church, I looked back and saw what I was looking for: Jeremiah. He stood by the coffin, his hand on the smooth metal surface.

I could almost see his lips form the word, "Goodbye."

CHAPTER FORTY-EIGHT

When we got back to the house, I stalled in the driveway. I couldn't go into that house, stay trapped inside my room.

"I'm going on a walk," I said.

Mom glanced at my heels and dress. "In that?"

I rubbed my arm and nodded.

"Be back soon," she said.

Without replying, I turned and started down my regular path to the beach where I'd been training for the marathon. When I hit the sandy edge, I slipped off my shoes and let my feet sink into the sand. The closer I got to the water's edge, the softer it felt.

Just like that morning I left for New York, I

found myself sitting on the sand, staring out over the ocean.

The waves rolled in, soft and lazy. The full moon was probably a couple weeks away. Would I still feel this way then?

I glanced down and caught sight of my tattoo which quickly blurred from my tears. I'd wanted to have something permanent to keep Greg with me. But no matter how much ink lay under my skin, he was gone.

Someone coughed behind me, hacking, and I turned to see who it was.

Karen stood about ten feet off, doubled over her knees, coughing.

I wiped at my eyes. "I don't know why you smoke." I said, remembering the horrible taste. It had taken brushing my teeth five times to get it out of my mouth.

"We all do things that hurt us sometimes," she said. "Smokin's mine."

I stared back over the water. She dropped down beside me in the sand, breathless.

"Why didn't you tell me you lost your job?" I asked, keeping my eyes ahead.

She let out a heavy sigh. "Didn't figure you needed any more to worry about."

That made me feel worse. I'd been so caught up in myself, Karen had to carry that weight in silence. I shook my head. "I'm sorry. I know you loved it."

"I did. But good things don't always last forever."

Wasn't that the truth. I sighed. "What are you doing out here?"

"Avoiding your parents."

I snorted. "Really?"

She laughed. "Kind of."

I didn't ask her what she meant.

"So, what's next in the life of Sydney Thane?"

"I can barely think past today." How could I be planning my future, college, relationships, when Greg had lost all of that?

"You better start," she said. "Because life's going to keep on moving whether you like it or not."

"This is different."

"No, it's not." She sounded angry, and I opened my eyes to look at her. Her stare felt heavier than everything else already sitting on my shoulders. "Did you hear what Jeremiah said back there? You can't keep letting your guilt hold you back."

I bristled because Jeremiah had said the same exact thing during our argument. "You don't know what I'm going through."

"You think the rest of us aren't hurting? Your parents, Jeremiah?"

"That's not—"

"No," Karen said. "No more excuses. You're just being a quitter. You're giving up."

The words hit me like a punch to the gut, and I bit my lip.

She stared over the water for second. "But you're quitting all the wrong things."

Shocked out of my pain for the briefest of seconds, I asked, "What?"

"You need to quit. Feelin' sorry for yourself. Blamin' yourself. Blamin' everyone else. Takin' on everyone else's problems. Maybe you should be a quitter, and then maybe you could finally bitch-slap pain in the face and stomp on its worthless nuts."

My mouth opened and closed while the thought of what she suggested wrestled with everything I'd gone through in the last four months. Who would I be without the weight of all that grief? Without it pressing on my shoulders, I could float away, disappear.

Her eyes held mine still as she grabbed my hands. "Are you ready to quit?"

Moisture pooled on my lids as I realized I was. More than anything, I wanted to stop feeling the way I felt right then. I wanted to do something that mattered, and I couldn't do it sitting on this beach.

CHAPTER FORTY-NINE

My parents hardly ever fought when we were growing up. Dad usually just gave in to what Mom wanted, tried to keep her happy. The longest argument they'd had was about whether or not Greg should play football in high school. He'd played in middle school and gotten beat up every single game because of his size, even to the point of breaking his arm.

Mom insisted he was too small and refused to let him play.

Dad said Greg could risk a broken arm—or whatever else—if he wanted to. Dad even went as far as saying he would sign the slip against Mom's wishes if she didn't give in by Friday.

For the rest of that week, Mom did nothing

around the house. No dishes, no cooking, no laundry, no scheduling, and no talking. It was torture. For all of us.

Finally, Dad opened the cabinet one morning looking for a bowl to pour himself some cereal for supper, but couldn't find one. Not even a coffee cup. Or a regular cup. Or a mixing bowl, Tupperware, or measuring cup. He looked. And then he caved.

"Damn it," he'd shouted. "Fine. He won't play football. Now will you start talking to us again, and I'll order some pizza?"

And then it ended. Mom helped us sign up for cross-country, and the rest was history.

But when I got home from sitting on the beach with Karen, I could hear them fighting, screaming, yelling things at each other that made my stomach turn.

Karen put a hand on my back. "Do you want to go somewhere else?"

I shook my head. I needed to do this, and going somewhere else to avoid their fight would just give me another excuse to quit the wrong thing.

No more excuses.

I pushed the door open and yelled out to them

before I could hear any more horrible things coming out their mouths.

Karen and I walked into the kitchen, where dishes were broken on the floor and my parents stood across the room from each other, red faced and breathing hard. I didn't know who had thrown the plates, but right now, it didn't matter.

"I'm leaving," I said. "I need to go to New York and run that race. For Greg and Liam. For me."

Mom and Dad stared at me.

"I thought we made it pretty clear you're not allowed," Mom said.

I shrugged. "Things have changed. I'm not your little girl anymore."

Dad folded his arms across his chest. "How are you going to get there?"

"I..." My mouth opened and closed.

Karen put her hand on my shoulder. "I'll take her."

Mom and Dad both stared at her.

"You know," Mom said, glaring at Karen but speaking to me, "the consequence still stands. If you leave, you can't come back."

My chest heaved. If I left now, I'd be homeless.

"Quit," Karen whispered to me, reminding me of our conversation on the beach.

That was all it took.

"I know," I said. "I'll figure something out." I didn't know how, but I would.

Mom pressed her fingers into her forehead and rubbed. "Sydney, it's been a hard day. Can you just go to your room, please? So your father and I can talk?"

I turned my eyes toward the ceiling and the fabric peeling from the roof. "No."

"Excuse me?"

"Mom, you and Dad are splitting up. That is your decision, and no matter how big of a mistake I think it is, I can't do anything about it. I'm almost eighteen, and it's time for me to make my own decisions. This thing—this race, it matters to me."

She tried to cut in, but I kept pressing on, talking over her. I had to get this out.

"This was the last thing Greg wanted to do, and he wanted to do it for Liam." I grit my teeth together to keep from crying out in pain. "Liam died yesterday, and there is no way I'm not running this race, in memory of him."

And I realized that was true. I would do

anything, leave anything, give up anything to be in New York, running that race. No matter what my parents said.

So I turned around and walked out of the house. I didn't turn around when she called the first, second, or third time.

Karen didn't turn around either. She just squeezed my hand, got in the car, and backed out of the driveway.

"That's my quitter," she said.

CHAPTER FIFTY

"Turn here," I said.
"But the freeway's that way."
"I know."

She turned to the right into the richest part of Sweet Water. My parents' house was big, but these were giant, with wide glass windows, perfectly landscaped lawns, and expensive cars sitting in the driveways even with five-car garages.

"Right there," I said, pointing out a white home with blue shutters and massive columns.

My heart fell to see Jeremiah's Jeep missing from the driveway. His parents must have locked it up and put it in the garage.

Karen pulled her battered car into the driveway, next to a gleaming BMW. "Is this the house I think it is?"

I nodded. "Wait here." I needed to see Jeremiah. It didn't feel right leaving for New York without him. And I needed to tell him that he was right. And that I was sorry. Yeah, I needed to stop blaming myself for Greg's death, but I needed to stop blaming Jeremiah too.

I walked down the smooth sidewalk, up the wooden front steps, and pressed the doorbell. I could hear it chiming through the house.

A few moments later, the peephole darkened and then the door swung open. His mom stood in the doorway, her arms folded over her chest, and she stared at me under her lash extensions.

"What are you doing here, Sydney?"

"I..." His mom never used to seem this intimidating, but now I had to dig my voice out from under her heavy stare. "Is Jeremiah here? I need to talk to him."

Her features remained a cold, hard mask. "He's not available right now."

"Do you know when he will be?"

"He's not available ever," she said and shut the door in my face.

I stared at the blue wood, blinking back tears.

CHAPTER 50

When I thought I had myself under control, I walked back to the car and got in.

Karen didn't ask me any questions, just started the drive.

Unlike the last time I was leaving Sweet Water, I wished that Jeremiah was the one sitting beside me.

CHAPTER FIFTY-ONE

Going on a road trip with Karen was way more uneventful than with Jeremiah. Even though her car looked like a rust bucket from the outside, it ran without breaking down, never ran out of gas, and didn't get flat tires. The cops even left us alone this time.

We drove straight through the day, only stopping for bathroom breaks or to pick up snacks. I'd need to be up and at the starting line to register at eight the next morning. It was late in the evening by the time we neared our destination.

The New York City skyline took my breath away. I stared at the lights and the signs and the cars whizzing past as we drove into the city.

Compared to Sweet Water, I could understand why they called it the City That Never Sleeps.

Karen booked a room for us near the marathon registration and went right to bed, but I couldn't sleep. Not yet.

"I'm going for a walk," I said.

"Be safe."

"I will." Whatever that meant.

Walking down the busy street, I didn't feel in danger at all. More like amazed that there were this many people in one place, still awake even though it was late and we'd been driving for ten hours and my world had fallen apart.

The emerald top of the Empire State Building caught my eye, and I stopped, staring it at. Was this how Dorothy felt in Oz?

Someone bumped into me and kept on walking like nothing had happened. Like they couldn't see the beauty of the building outlined against the black sky.

This had been here my whole life, but I was just now seeing it, and I wanted to take it all in.

I kept walking down the sidewalk, looking in shops, watching couples holding hands, and feeling lonely myself.

Stairs rose to my right, and I read a sign that

said The High Line. It was a park that used to be a railway. I let my feet carry me up the lit path and marveled at the little oasis in the middle of the city, but my heart still ached.

Jeremiah was supposed to be here with me.

He should have been showing me all his favorite spots since his family used to come here all the time. He probably knew the best bakeries and pizza shops and all the things that were classically New York.

Mostly, I missed the things that were classically Jeremiah. Even here with countless landmarks, museums, and incredible views, the real sight I wanted to see was those beautiful brown eyes, gleaming under endless city lights.

That smile that made even the Statue of Liberty's torch seem dim.

Those fingers wrapped around mine even though they could have been holding any other hand.

Those lips asking me if I was ready.

I could have looked him up online, stared at his picture until my battery died, but Jeremiah was kind of like that sunrise on the ferry. No photo could ever do him justice.

Instead of wallowing even more, I did what I

did best. I put one foot in front of the other. I didn't stop until I made it to the room where Karen quietly snored, and I lay in bed, becoming one of the reasons why New York City is the city that never sleeps.

CHAPTER FIFTY-TWO

Karen didn't need to wake me up in the morning. No, my eyes were wide open at 4:48 a.m., staring at the ceiling that never fully got dark, even with the curtains drawn.

Her blankets rustled as she rolled over and shifted. We had twelve minutes before we needed to get up and get ready. I would dress in running clothes, make sure my fanny pack was stocked. Then, we'd go and eat a breakfast full of protein and healthy fats, sure to give me energy for 26.2 miles.

The thought made me shudder. Twenty-six miles. I'd never run that far before, but the expert who'd designed the training program said that was fine. Anyone who followed the workouts would be ready.

I took in a deep breath. I could do this. I'd been through worse.

A deep hole in my chest reminded me that it was just Karen and me. I wished Jeremiah was here with Bubby and Hoolie. I wished that he would walk me as close as he could to the starting line and ask, "Are you ready?" with those adventure eyes.

I closed my eyes for a second and opened them again. I needed to give up on impossible dreams.

The alarm clock on the nightstand chimed, and Karen's spindly hand dropped onto the button. She rubbed her eyes and swung her feet over the edge of the bed.

After she'd taken a few deep breaths and coughed, she went outside. I imagined the whole of New York City getting to see her in her nightgown and fuzzy socks, inhaling like her life depended on it.

The thought brought a smile to my face.

While she was outside, I went and showered, then got dressed.

The action seemed too simple, but I supposed the marathon would be too. All I'd have to do was put one foot in front of the other until I reached the end.

I went on a short walk while she showered and got dressed, and then we left. My stomach tied itself into a million knots while I tried to eat, but I forced some food down. I would need my energy.

We paid, left, and made our way through the city to the starting line. As the crowd of people got thicker and thicker, my anxiety grew.

Karen stood by me for as long as she could, helped me pin my number on my shirt, but then it was time to say goodbye.

She put her hands on my shoulders and looked me in the eyes. "Have I ever told you how amazing you are?"

My lips twitched as I shook my head.

She brushed her thumb over my chin. "I know you always felt like you were living in Greg's shadow, but I've always seen a spark in you." Karen tilted her head toward the crowd of people lining up. "Now I get to watch it become a flame."

I smiled.

"Greg would be proud of you."

I didn't have any words for that, so I just hugged her tight. "Thank you."

CHAPTER FIFTY-THREE

I'd never felt as alone as I did standing in a crowd of thousands of people, waiting to run the marathon. As other runners brushed past me, laughed, chatted with each other, shared how nervous they were, I pretended to be busy. I tucked my phone in my fanny pack, made sure the zippers were completely closed. But no matter how busy my hands were, they couldn't compete with my busy mind.

I couldn't help but think that Greg should have been the one here, running the race. That it would have meant so much to him to be this close to fulfilling his promise to Liam. I wondered if he could see me now, and if so, what he thought. Would he be proud, like Karen said? Happy?

I could only hope.

Someone called my name from the sidelines. Three someones. What were Bubby and Hoolie doing with Karen? I wanted to go talk to them, but the announcer came over the speaker, saying the race would be starting soon.

They waved at me, and I smiled and gave them a thumbs up. Karen must have told them we had changed our minds. I couldn't believe they had come to watch me run.

"Fancy meeting you here."

That couldn't be.

I spun, and there stood Jeremiah, looking at me like we were the only two people in all of Manhattan.

"What are you doing here?" I asked.

His eyes scanned the crowd for a moment, but it was obvious he wasn't really seeing them. "I was sitting in my room, by myself, while my dad was at work and my mom was at the country club, and I thought, are those the people I need to please? I made a promise back in January to myself, to Greg, and to Liam that I would run this marathon."

My mouth fell open. "But..."

"I was on my way out of town when I saw you alongside the road. It was like…fate."

Something dawned on me. "Your parents. They found out because of your credit card. You never signed up for the senior trip, did you?"

He shook his head, then lifted his shirt.

My gaze trailed up the toned muscles of his side and landed on a tattoo. 26.2. "I was going to run it for him."

I wiped tears away from my eyes. "Jere, I'm sorry. I tried to go by your house and tell you—I shouldn't have treated you the way I did."

"Sydney," he said, "I know I messed up at the party. I should have gone about my feelings for you the right way, but I can't go back. I can only tell you that right here, right now, I'll be there for you every single painful, difficult, messy, impossible step of the way."

Our lips met somewhere in the middle, and he held me close to his chest. And I let him, because I needed to let myself be happy, to live my life even when I was scared or sad or guilty.

"In ten, nine…" the announcer boomed over the loudspeakers.

Jeremiah broke apart from our kiss, still cupping my cheeks in his hands. "Are you ready?"

I put every part of myself into my answer. "Yes."

CHAPTER FIFTY-FOUR

Running the marathon had been hard, but we both knew our race was far from over. We had to learn how to stop keeping the pace and to start striding ahead. That started the very next morning when our bodies ached and sported blisters the size of which we'd never seen before.

I could have slept for three days straight, but life got in the way. I had to drive home—if I even had a home—get ready for school and track tryouts the next day. Just like Aunt Karen had been trying to tell me, I needed to think of my future. Time would move on with or without me.

After packing our things, Karen and I were meeting Jeremiah and his grandparents at a bagel

CHAPTER 54

place in Queens, near where they'd stayed with a family friend. I drove. As I watched the city pass outside my window, it struck me how different it was, just from one block to another. Maybe my next adventure could be in New York?

A smile touched my lips. A dream. I could live with that.

We had to park at least a mile away from the shop, but it was good because it helped me stretch my legs out.

The closer we got, the faster my heart beat. I wanted to see *him*.

We reached the shop window, and I looked in. There he was, with Bubby and Hoolie, sipping coffee, with a tired, serene look. I took in every inch of him. Could this be real? Could he be mine?

Karen put her arm around my waist. "You got a real creepy vibe goin' on, hon."

I laughed and went to the front door. As the five of us ate breakfast, my heart felt broken but fuller than it had in a long, long time. These five people loved each other, supported each other, told each other the truth, even when it was hard. That was special.

And hard to say goodbye to.

But we did.

We all parted ways at the door, Jere and I walking to his Jeep, Bubby and Hoolie going to their car, and Karen going to hers.

When Jere and I buckled into our seats, he looked over at me. And since there weren't any words for that moment, I leaned in and pressed my lips to his. Kisses had a million flavors, but this one was sweet, tired, loving, and it said the words we couldn't come up with just then.

On the drive home, Jeremiah and I took turns sleeping and driving. This time, the top was up, but I still curled into Bubby's blanket. I tried not to think of what was coming for me when I got home. Mom hadn't called or texted since Karen and I left.

The ten-hour drive passed more quickly than I wanted it to. When Jeremiah pulled along the curb in front of my house, Mom's car was the only one in the driveway.

"You can do this," he said.

I pulled a corner of my lip back. "What about you?"

He shrugged. "I think Hoolie talked to my dad. He's taking next weekend off and has a two-week-long vacation planned for after graduation."

CHAPTER 54

A dream come true for Jeremiah.

I squeezed his hand. "That's great."

He nodded. "Call me when you get everything sorted. If not, we'll take it from there."

"I will," I said, trying not to think about the if not.

I didn't hear his Jeep pull away until I was at the front door. I almost knocked, but thought better of it. My key still worked, so I let myself in.

Walking through the front door stopped me in my tracks.

Greg smiled back at me from the mantel, the walls, a frame on the coffee table. I covered my mouth and walked through the living room to the dining room, taking in every one of the photos. And as I did, one of the million weights on my shoulders shattered, falling silently to the ground.

"Sydney?" Mom said from behind me.

I turned toward her. "The pictures?"

She looked at one hanging in the dining room and smiled softly. "I think you and I might have a lot in common. We run from our feelings."

I couldn't reply over the lump building in my throat.

"Your dad moved out last night, and I thought of what Jeremiah said. That we should live our lives through the pain and the guilt. It hurts to have your brother gone, it hurts to watch you suffer, but most of all, it hurts to feel like I've lost both of you."

Mom rubbed her arm. "So I'm hoping you'll stay here, until graduation, and then we can both start our new lives, somewhere else."

I smiled through the tears and took her in a hug. Dad may have moved out, but I had my mom, and she had me.

CHAPTER FIFTY-FIVE

Jeremiah picked me up early the next morning. We had something to do before our first class back at school.

We made a stop at the store to get a photo of us at the finish line. After typing the next address into his phone, he started to a house across town from ours while I added the photo to the scrapbook, over the top of my letter to Liam.

Jeremiah slowed on residential streets. These houses were smaller than the ones we lived in, but the yards were full of big, untrimmed flower bushes and plastic kids' toys. Full of life.

One house looked just like the rest, but we knew the pain that lay inside.

Jeremiah looked over the home, sadness in his eyes.

I felt connected to Liam's family in that moment. I understood what it felt like to look normal on the outside but crumble on the inside.

"Come on," I said and got out of the car.

I carried the giftbag to the front door, and when Jeremiah stood beside me, I knocked. While we waited, I listened to the TV playing the morning news.

The volume went down, and the door swung open, revealing Liam's mom looking thin and small in her sweats.

"Sydney," she said, lightening a little. "Jeremiah. Come in."

"We can't stay long," I said. "We have to get to school, but we wanted to bring this by."

She stepped on the porch and gingerly took the bag from me. Nerves fired through my stomach as she reached in and pulled out the scrapbook. Her eyes watered at the photo of Liam and Greg on the front.

"I was going to give this to Liam." I scratched at my wrist. "I thought you should have it."

She hugged it to her chest with one arm and

pulled me in with the other. "Thank you so much, for all you did for him."

I shook my head against her shoulder. "We loved him so much."

We broke apart, and her eyes fixed on both of us. "He loved you two so much."

A quiet fell over us for a moment until Jere said we should get to school.

"Good luck," she said, then looked at me. "Tell your mom I'll call her tomorrow."

Confusion made me furrow my brows.

"She gave me her number at the funeral."

That's what that scrap of paper was. "I will tell her." I smiled. "We'll see you later."

At least I knew she had Mom and Mom had her. They had one of the worst tragedies in common, but it was something.

Once we got in the car, Jeremiah said, "One more stop."

He didn't need directions for this one. We'd both been here before. Soon, we were driving under the sign that said Sweet Water Cemetery and parking in one of the many empty spots.

Jeremiah reached up and took our marathon medals off the rearview mirror and walked with me to Liam's grave where grass hadn't even started growing through the freshly turned dirt.

A picture of him smiled at us from the gravestone adorned with flowers. Even in black and white, it shined. Beneath his picture, a line in slanted text said, "Watch a sunrise, for me."

Jere held out one of the medals and gave it to me. With my throat burning, I kneeled down and hung it over the corner of his stone. "We did it," I said.

Jeremiah rubbed my shoulder, letting me know he was here, even on this messy step.

I stood up and took a deep breath. We weren't done yet.

We walked farther down the cemetery trail, nearing the end of this emotional marathon. The closer we got to Greg's gravestone, the weaker my legs felt. Just like in the actual race, Jeremiah put his arm around my waist and supported me in our final steps. I fell across the finish line and knelt at Greg's grave, everything in me spent.

A dark spot formed on the cement base of Greg's headstone as Jere knelt beside me. Thick tears spilled over his eyelashes.

He laid the medal over Greg's grave and held

me close to him. "We did it," Jere said. "We made it."

As we held each other, weeping over my brother's grave, I realized we *had* made it. We were moving on with our lives and starting something new, but a piece of us would always be here in Sweet Water. Maybe that was a good thing. If we ever got lost, we could always find our way back to each other.

EPILOGUE

Jeremiah fit the last of my things into his Jeep. We'd managed to fill the trunk, the back seat, and even a cargo tub on top. This time, he had the hard shell on.

Beside us in the driveway, there was a big enclosed trailer with boxes and furniture going to my mom and Karen's new place. Mom used her half of the money from the sale of the house to buy a smaller place farther from the beach, and since Karen got a new job selling motorcycles in Sweet Water, they were going to room together, at least for now.

Mom came to stand beside us. "You drive safe with my daughter, you understand?"

"Yes, ma'am," Jere said.

Her expression softened. "I can't believe you two are going to college."

I couldn't either. Just like Aunt Karen had said, life kept moving forward, whether I was ready for it or not.

"Just a couple months and I'll be coming to your first cross-country meet," she commented, excitement in her eyes.

"I can't wait," I said.

She wrapped me in a hug. "I love you so much."

I hugged her and whispered the words back. These last couple of months had been hard, but she'd let go, let me live my life.

Dad? Not so much. But then again, some people let loss stop their lives. I'd been there.

"We better get going," Jere said. "Don't wanna be late for the barbecue."

Another freshman barbecue. But this time, Jere and I would be attending as friends. More than that.

"Have fun," Mom said, wiping at her eyes, making moisture form in my own.

We both knew these weren't normal leaving tears. Greg should have been going with Jere and me, but that wasn't life. We would have to live with that fact always, learn to accept that the future didn't look like what we'd hoped for. That was our life. I didn't understand it, didn't have to like it, but I had come to terms with it. For now. Another wave of grief would knock me down soon enough, but I'd have to get right back up.

I went to Mom again and hugged her tight. "You know Greg would have been making some joke right now to cheer you up."

She laughed a little through the tears. "You're right."

"Love you, Mom."

She held my cheek and rubbed her thumb over my cheekbone. "Love you, precious girl."

Jeremiah and I got into the Jeep.

"Are you ready?" he asked with those adventure eyes.

"No." I pressed a button on his radio. Greg's favorite song started playing, and I turned it up. "Now I am."

Jeremiah held my hand and started driving. As we pulled away from my home, our old lives, I had no idea what our futures would hold, but right now I was glad I had Jeremiah. So much had changed since I decided to take a road trip with my enemy. My parents had divorced and I'd lost a friend, but I'd gained a boyfriend. Someone to love me through it all, every single messy step of the way.

Sign up for Kelsie Stelting's email newsletter to learn about new releases, special discounts, and exclusive fan content!

KEEP READING IN SWEET
WATER HIGH

Check out the next book in the Sweet Water High Series!

My first kiss was an epic fail. But maybe he can make the next one better…

Start reading The Kissing Tutor today!

Other Sweet Water High Books
Misunderstanding the Billionaire's Heir by Anne-Marie Meyer
Crushing on My Brothers' Best Friend by Julia Keanini
Kissing the Boy Next Door by Judy Corry
Flirting with the Bad Boy by Michelle Pennington
Chemistry of a Kiss by Kimberly Krey
Falling for My Nemesis by Tia Kerch Souders
Falling for My Best Friend by Victorine Leiske
Much Ado About a Boy by Jeanette Lewis
Road Trip with the Enemy by Kelsie Stelting
The Kissing Tutor by Sally Henson

ALSO BY KELSIE STELTING

The Pen Pal Romance Series

Dear Adam

Stuck in the Friend Zone

Sincerely Cinderella

To My Perfect Guy (box set)

The Texas Star Series

Lonesome Skye: Book One

Becoming Skye: Book Two

Loving Skye: Book Three

Always Anika

Abi and the Boy Next Door

Other YA Contemporary Romance

The Art of Taking Chances

Road Trip with the Enemy

The Texas Sun Series

All the Things He Left Behind

Unfair Catch: Savannah's Story 1

Anything But Yes: Savannah's Story 2

Nonfiction

Raising the West

AUTHOR'S NOTE

Sometimes you can't see how far you've come until you reach the top of the mountain. Grief is kind of like that. You're sad and miss the person you lost. You think of them every day. You cry. A lot. And then one day you wake up and realize it's been a few days since you cried, since you wanted to call their number in your phone.

No matter how many people you lose, though, it doesn't get easier. Knowing death is a part of life doesn't make it easier.

As you read this, you're probably thinking of someone. A grandparent, family member, friend…I know I am.

If you're suffering from loss, I know there's not much I can tell you other than it gets better.

Someday, you'll look up, and like Aunt Karen said, you'll bitch-slap grief in the face and step on its nuts. You'll decide to live your life, because in the end, your life, your memories, your relationships, are all you have that actually matters.

Make it count.

ACKNOWLEDGMENTS

Being included in the Sweet Water High Series is a massive blessing. I am thankful to the organizers for including me in the list of talented authors to bring this series to life. Working with the organizers and other authors was a fun, collaborative experience.

As I wrote this—working on a tight deadline—my husband gave me the space to get up early every morning to get my words in. I'm so thankful to him and his endless supply of support.

My author friend, Sally Henson, helped me work through some of the tougher parts of drafting. Having her a phone call or Facebook message away made all the difference.

My family will always be listed in this section

of the book for how wonderfully supportive they are. I love writing, knowing I have a cheering section for as long as I live.

Victorine Leiske designed the covers for the series, and I'm thankful she gave my book and the others a beautiful cover.

Someone once told me a good editor is worth their weight in gold, but I'm pretty sure my editor, Tricia Harden, is worth at least twice that.

As always, thank you to you, the reader. I hope you fell in love with this world enough to share the magic with someone else.

ABOUT THE AUTHOR

Kelsie Stelting grew up in the middle of nowhere (also known as western Kansas). Her rural upbringing taught her how to get her hands dirty and work hard for what she believes in. Kelsie loves writing honest fiction that readers can vacation in, as well as traveling, volunteering, ice cream, loving on her family, and soaking up just a little too much sun wherever she can find it.

To connect with Kelsie, email her at kelsie@kelsiestelting.com or join Kelsie Stelting: Readers Club on Facebook.

- facebook.com/kelsiesteltingcreative
- instagram.com/kelsiestelting
- bookbub.com/authors/kelsie-stelting
- goodreads.com/goodreadscomkelsiestelting

Made in the USA
Monee, IL
13 August 2021